THE GHOSTS OF TRITON

The Ghosts of Triton

The Solar Colonies 2

Ken Catran

Hodder
Children's
Books

a division of Hodder Headline plc

Contents

AD 2044

Prologue

In the first decade of the twenty-first century, Earth is decimated by plague, pollution and a stripped ozone layer. The mineral resources of outer space are urgently needed and full solar colonisation begins.

Human bodies are not designed for outer space. So 'new humans' are created, their bodies genetically adjusted to the different pressures of outer space; then Earth tints these gene colonists different skin colours to keep them separated. On North-West Mars they are blue-skinned and blue-haired; in the North-East they are green-skinned and green-haired. On the asteroids, rich in the resources needed by a pollution-stricken Earth, a strong, tough race of miners is created, red-brown in skin and hair colour.

Blue Martians and green Martians dislike each other, but are all 'Sandies' after the oceans of sand that sweep Mars. Mars can be terraformed into a living planet, but not the asteroid rocks colonised by the red-brown 'Rockies'. To Earth, all solar colonists – 'Solies' or 'Tints' – blue, green or red, are workers and second-class citizens created to serve Earth.

But now the second generation of colonists has an identity of its own. Earth is just another planet in the heavens. The new generation wants to make life better on the colonised planets. The years of isolation are coming to a flash-point.

On Earth's solar frontier, the fires of independence are flickering to life. Our story happens in AD 2044.

1 Terror on a cold rock

Aliens. The word dropped into Dexter's thoughts like an ice-cube, sudden, sharp-edged and tinkling, and the power cut on his laser drill. Dex made the metal face of his android-remote look round. But there was nothing; through his visor-screen eyes, the icy blue wastelands of Triton stretched in all directions and Dex could almost feel the freezing cold. He had to keep telling himself that only his thought lock was in this android on Neptune's moon of Triton, and that he was controlling it from a console chair and virtual reality on a space station orbiting the planet Mars.

But why did he suddenly think about aliens?

Nerves, he told himself; nobody has ever met an alien and nobody ever will. He thought-powered his bronze-fingered hand to press the starting control again as a flurry of pink-coloured snow swirled past. The temperature on Triton was minus 400° and a human body would freeze solid within a second. But directing his thought power into the android was so real that there was no feeling of Mars at all – he was here on Triton with three other cadets, setting up an automatic mining probe. He pressed the starting control again, but the laser refused to flicker into life.

'Dexter, why have you stopped?' came Control's voice in his ear-circuits. It was a calm and steady voice, but Romhilda could just as calmly demerit him, so Dex answered quickly.

'My drill is dead – maybe it needs a new battery.'

'Wait, Dexter.' The channel clicked off again.

Dex waited. All his awareness was in the android as though he was standing in its metal skin, projected across the millions of black space kilometres from Mars on ultrasonic wavelengths. And waiting made him nervous because it made him think about an accident – a 'bounce' that would fuse his thought waves back too quickly into his body on Mars and damage his brain. It was a risk and a bad one, but if he wanted a fast-track to seniority, then he had to take his chances. The other three android-remotes had already noticed he was standing still.

'She's checking your battery, Dex. Another demerit if you fused the drill.' Tieve's voice teased on their communication as his android face turned, the dark light glinting wickedly off the bronze features.

'Romhilda doesn't trust anyone,' came Phyllida's voice. Her android was on its knees in the blue ice, fitting a tripod leg in place. 'Least of all you, Dex.'

She was teasing too, and Dex ignored her. He thought-directed his metal fingers to loosen slightly round the handle of the drill; it was always incredible to watch this, even more to realise he was 'standing' on the surface of Triton, Neptune's largest moon and twenty-six million kilometres from Mars. His mind was locked into an android circuit brain and he was directing it to set the probe in place.

Another flurry of snow from Triton's ice-cap splattered itself across the bronze-skinned android body and Dex groaned. The weather was closing again and there would be more delays, more risk because they were getting more and more of that pink-coloured snow. And not for the first time, Dex asked himself *which* genius on Earth decided this base had to be so close to the ice-cap? Romhilda's cold voice buzzed in his ear-circuits again.

'Battery flat.'

'Can't be. I plugged in a new one,' yelled Dex angrily.

'Change it,' came her disbelieving tones. 'Fault noted.'

Any damned excuse to give me a hard time thought Dex, already thought-turning his android body to walk over. Her voice buzzed in his ear-circuits again.

'Respond correctly, Cadet Dexter.'

'Copy your instruction, Control. Changing batteries.'

'And move it,' snapped the third android – Conleth. 'Let's get the tripods in before cut-off.'

'Go scramble yourself,' muttered Dex as he directed his metal hands to unclip and exchange the unit. Then out of nowhere, the word came back into his mind. Aliens. And Dex remembered that the power had cut the same moment as he had thought it. Now, just for a moment, it was as though a huge invisible eye was watching him. Then the snow thickened and something moved. Dex looked over and gaped for a horrified moment at the thing coming towards him, out of the pink flurry.

'Control, I have an alien life form on visual— '

'Disconnect,' buzzed Romhilda's voice at once.

The pink snow was thick round Dex, screening him from the other androids. He was moving backwards, stumbling a little as the thing came towards him. 'Wait, I think I can get a better look— '

'Disconnect, Dexter!'

5

The disconnect speared through his brain and his head jarred painfully against the sides of the helmet as the power charge jolted off. Now he could feel his seated body in the chair unit, the helmet electrodes digging into his forehead. He flicked a side-switch with his finger and the helmet slid up from his face.

He sank his head back into the padded headrest of the chair. Ahead, the monitor in front of the helmet was freeze-framed in a mass of pink Triton snow. Dex's head was pounding painfully, the way it always did when the signal disconnected abruptly, and he rubbed his hands over his face. Beside him, the other helmets had risen and Conleth groaned.

'Bouncing can't be any worse,' he muttered. 'Dex, what did you tell Romhilda?'

I saw something alien in the snow, Dex made to say, but already it was sounding too ludicrous. There were no aliens, *anywhere*, so why had he reacted like that? There was disbelief and even anger in the voices of the other three now as they sat up in their chairs.

'Aliens, Dex?' Tieve, his brown hair in long curls. He made to speak again and Romhilda's voice cut round them.

'Sit tight, we're scanning from the tel-spark.' She sounded grim and very angry and her vision screen stayed blank.

'Aliens?' Conleth got out of his chair and stretched himself. 'Little green ones or bug-eyed monsters? Anyway, thanks for the break.'

'Did you really see something, Dex?' Phyllida had very calculating green eyes and her black hair was in a close cut round her face.

'Something.' Dex stopped, he didn't even believe

6

himself now. An alien something with goggle eyes and a tube mouth. But things like that belonged in the Earth comics of last century. Not here today, on a spoke station orbiting Mars in the year 2044.

'Get yourself a coffee,' said Tieve unsympathetically.

Dex stood up. The control room was set with different shades of light and dark blue and ahead, past their chairs and consoles, a long observation window curved out. On both sides extended a massive tube arm of the giant spoke-wheeled space station. Below, half in shadow, hung the red planet of Mars. Dex was a very small part of this super-big Mars Orbit and he had never felt smaller. Romhilda would talk to Jahudi, senior controller for mining remotes, and that was *all* he needed. His head still hurt. Phyllida smiled an unkind grin, too, as she pushed a coffee into his hand.

'You spooked on a double-image – admit it,' she said.

Dex always had an answer ready, but not today. He could still see that thing, half-seen and horrible in the drifting pink snow, and the image wouldn't go away.

'Mars link!' shouted Tieve suddenly.

A side monitor screen flashed on in response to his voice-link. Two girls, teenagers like them, sat at a big powerful console. Both were strong-built with red-brown hair and red-brown faces. The first girl turned a closed hostile face at them.

'Did you over-boost our Triton signal?' Unconsciously, Tieve's voice took on that sharp adult-to-child tone he always used when talking to Martian colonists.

'No,' the girl snapped. The name ASA was black-lettered on her dark-red smock.

'Rockies?' Phyllida had joined them. Her voice carried clearly through the two-way communication. 'What do they know?'

The girl scowled. 'Go bounce yourselves,' she snapped, and the screen went abruptly blank.

'And you, sweetie,' muttered Conleth. 'Rockies on Marsbase – what next?' He jumped as Romhilda's voice sounded around them.

'Cadets, scans are negative for alien life-form. Repeat, negative. Get back under your Copy helmets.' Dex turned with the others and thought for a moment he'd got away with it. Then Romhilda's voice continued, 'Not you, Dexter.'

Tieve grinned and Phyllida made a little throat-cutting gesture but they moved quickly back to their consoles. There was always real authority in Romhilda's calm voice. The others were just under their helmets, systems lights flashing, when behind them the big end screen came to life.

'Dexter.'

He turned round, remembering to look respectful. Romhilda was on-screen, projected from her control centre on the top tier. She was tall with red-tinted black hair in plaits round a face that was serious and strong, like a chubby apple. She sat back and clasped her hands, waiting just long enough to make him nervous.

'Dexter, standing orders are to disconnect Copies upon alien sighting.'

'Yes, Control.'

'Of course there has never been a confirmed alien sighting, but standing orders are standing orders – right?'

'Yes, Control.'

Behind him, the system lights on the other three

8

helmets were shining. Their bodies might be seated in those chairs but their very brains were mind-linked back to Triton and he knew exactly what they would be doing – quietly sniggering and making their android-remotes give bronze thumbs-up to each other at the sight of his own android standing motionless under the dark Triton sky. Romhilda was still speaking.

'Of course, sometimes a new cadet freaks and thinks he or she has seen one— '

'Control, I— '

'Or,' she continued like a steam-roller, 'sometimes it's a useful way of getting a coffee break.' Romhilda had very blue eyes in her black face and they rested on the coffee cup Dex was still holding. 'I call *that* kind of cadet by an old Earth-name: smartass. Know what it means?'

'Yes Control, but— '

'Demerit, Dexter.'

'Yes, Control.' That makes the lucky dozen he thought bitterly, one month longer out here!

Romhilda sighed. 'Dexter, your attitude problem is boring. How did you ever get to Spoke – let alone Mars Orbit?'

Probably because you weren't grading me, thought Dex, but to himself because Romhilda used a big stick. He was enough demerits down already. 'I'm sorry Control, I'll work an extra hour on my shift to make up.'

'No.' Romhilda's plaits shook with her head. Behind her was a big telescreen hologram of Earth showing the immense crystal dome of Pacific City. Real sunlight sparkled on the glass and real white clouds drifted overhead. 'Dexter, you are controlling

9

android-remotes on a moon of Neptune, just about as far out as we've ever worked. You must project yourself, think, act and *be* that Copy. It needs the skill, the reflex and the strength of young brains. Unfortunately that also carries the problems of youth.'

The same sermon, thought Dex, and tried a new move, humility. 'I understand, Control,' he said meekly. 'Thank you for the advice.' It was spoiled, though, by the cup of coffee he was still holding.

'Remember it.'

'Yes, Control.' He decided it was worth a try. 'Any chance of forgetting my demerit?'

'Remember that word I used?'

'Yes, Control.'

'Get back under your helmet.' Her lips framed 'smartass' again.

Dex slipped himself back into his console chair and put a hand on the helmet-control switch. Then the room cut with a loud, flinching sonic hum and he heard Tieve's voice again, not amused now but screaming with panic.

'Alien sighting – we're being attacked!'

2 The blue-ice nightmare

Now the control alarms were flashing and the Copy monitors starring and splitting as that sonic buzz screamed to a new high. Dex was sitting there, frozen, when out of the monitor static he saw that alien goggle-tube face again. And then, beside him, Conleth began to shake and jerk under his helmet like a helpless doll and Dex knew what had happened. Their thought waves were locked and they could not escape the electronic reality of Triton.

'Dexter! Keep away from your helmet!'

He turned in his seat. Romhilda was standing out of her chair, reaching across as though she wanted to grab him, frantically stabbing at her controls. But the sonic hum increased again, splitting up her picture, making her look funny and absurd. And beside him, his friends were jerking helplessly. He pulled the helmet down and slipped the electrode strap tight. That little click as it sealed, Romhilda's last shout lost in the building hum, then his mind hit the Copy wavelength and he was on Triton.

Just for a moment, but a moment of nightmare, silver-blue ice crunched underfoot and the pink snow was back in heavy swirls. Beside him, a Copy – Conleth's – crashed down. Then the tripod leg fell away, the probe crashed over and in the snow flurries, something two-legged and humanoid was standing there, tube-snouted, goggle-eyed and holding a strange pointed thing. Then a strong crashing surge of power seared like a black flood through his brain. The thing they all feared – bouncing!

The black flood was searing into red, clutching his brain like electronic flaming fingers. Now his eyes seemed on fire and his whole awareness split in the red, black-starred light. Through it, he could still see that horrible humanoid thing. Then, with a last splitting flash, Dex felt his head bash against the helmet. His thought-waves signal had somehow got itself back to Mars. Painful red flashes still cut like razors in front of his eyes, his head pounded in big painful thuds and from somewhere, far away, he could hear a tiny voice.

'Dexter – Dexter.'

It was Romhilda's voice and it grew louder. Dex made his helmet rise and looked at his monitor screen. It was blank and so were the screens beside it. He made himself get up and turn round, his body aching, his legs like wet paper. Romhilda's end screen was back in full hologramic reality and she was glaring at him.

'Get their helmets up.'

Dex nodded. He staggered over to Conleth's chair and hit the button. Up came the shiny big helmet and Conleth's head fell forward. His eyes were shut and the mind-wave readouts on his console flickered like dying sparks. Then Phyllida the same, and Tieve. His blond curls were round his face and his limp hand fell off the armrest. His readouts flickered and levelled.

The room was utterly silent. Dex knew Romhilda was watching, but he couldn't make himself look at her. His three companions slumped in their chairs as though asleep and he knew the base medics would be here soon. Also that there was almost nothing they could do.

'If you had stayed off-channel, maybe I could have unscrambled their signals.' Romhilda's voice was like cold iron. 'But you had to be a . . .' her voice lowered but Dex heard all too clearly, the next cutting word '. . . smartass.'

Now the black and red pain was flooding through Dex's head again. He shut his eyes and heard someone groan. It was him groaning, he knew that, but it was his last clear thought as the pain went to total black and he fell forward into a door-slamming silence.

When the darkness began unswirling into lighter colours, Dex was lying down flat. The sonic bandage round his head had lessened the terrible headache and when he opened his eyes, he glimpsed a light and dark green leaf pattern on the ceiling overhead. He was back in his cubicle, lying on his bed. He could move his hands and feet and that meant he wasn't bounced – that whiplashing power surge that would have made such a mess of his brain.

Dex groaned and shut his eyes again. Coming to Mars had seemed like a good idea when he let Friedelinde talk him into it; he was always letting Friedelinde talk him into things.

Earth needed a mineral supply now that its own was exhausted. And only in space could vulcanite be found, the new metal that lasted forever and kept out the worst solar radiation. But it was getting harder to find. The colonists on Mars and the asteroid bases of Pallas and Ceres wanted it for their own settlements, so Earth had to push further into the outer rim of planets – Saturn, Uranus, Neptune and their moons. The distances were so great that android Copies were sent, programmed and controlled by locking a strong young mind into a console helmet and sparking across space into the circuit brains of the Copy.

So that meant every 'Copy-capper', as they were nicknamed, risked that terrible searing flashback, the bounce that could scramble their brains like eggs inside the shell. And now it had happened. His friends were unconscious, in a coma they might never come out of. He heard himself groan again, then heard a voice speaking insistently.

'Dexter.'

He knew that voice and nearly didn't open his eyes again. But he also knew it wouldn't go away – and it didn't.

'Dexter!'

'You know I don't like being called Dexter,' he muttered as he sat up.

Friedelinde smiled. 'It has more dignity than Dex. Only Sandies and Rockies have short names, you know.'

'Are we having this conversation, Friedelinde? Do you *know* what's happened?'

'Yes, Dexter, I do.'

She was sitting cross-legged on a stool, practically at the end of his bunk. The pale tinted walls of her own bedroom shimmered round her. She had the new flower-patch make-up on her cheeks; her blouse and big floppy slacks were made of the new hologram silk. They changed from pink to red to yellow as she moved.

'Everything about you changes,' he muttered.

Friedelinde shook her blonde top-knot and it turned auburn. 'What I feel for you is the same,' she said sweetly, smiling. Her teeth went from white to gold. 'Dex, I've only got a minute, so listen— '

'Have to wait,' he muttered.

'It won't wait.' A sharp edge came into her voice. 'Listen, there has to be an inquiry, but it was a bounce, one of those Rockies on Marsbase did it.'

'What?' Dex sat up.

'A Rockie overboosted the signal and it blew back.' Her top-knot flopped and changed into a deep chestnut as she leaned forward, her eyes intent. 'That's what happened, Dex, that's the *official* story— '

'I saw something,' he said, his words still catching.

'Double-image, trauma, whatever, it happened when the signal overboosted. You'll get your hand smacked for interfering, that's all.'

'My hand smacked!' he yelled.

'Yes. Just get the story straight then I'll make sure Daddy gets you back to Earth and a sea city. Dex, remember— '

The wall-screen image flickered, vanished and was replaced by Romhilda. Dex didn't know how many hours had passed since he lost consciousness, but she looked exactly the same, even to her neat grey and black uniform with the green tabs of her senior rank. He got up, pulling his tunic more neatly into place. That was the worst about full-screen end walls – Control could visit you any time, even if you were changing underwear.

'Feeling better?' Her face looked like a cold apple.

'Yes, Control.'

'Did I interrupt an Earth-link?'

'No matter, Control.' You know damn well you did, he thought. Get on with it.

'The lovely Friedelinde, perhaps?'

'How are the others?' he yelled.

'Coma.' Romhilda's voice softened a little. 'On their way back to Earth.' She paused a moment, her blue eyes very remote. 'I take it you can remember what happened.'

You were monitoring Friedelinde, thought Dex. All right if you all want to play games, then it's not my problem. He nodded carefully.

'You were talking about something on Triton earlier. We've checked the visuals up to the moment everything blew. No trace.'

'No.' That tube-snouted goggle-eyed thing was still clear and he shut his eyes tight for a moment, trying to make it go away. 'No, it must have been double-image.'

'And did you see anything when you patched back, *against* my orders?' Romhilda's voice was careful and flat, the cold look firmly in place on her chubby, strong face.

'No, I didn't.' Dex shut his eyes again because he *had* seen something and a new voice spoke before he opened them again.

'You admit interrupting Romhilda's control of the emergency?'

It was the one voice he didn't want to hear. It was a smooth, whispering voice that had all the silent power of a rocket engine. And Dex knew before he opened his eyes that the voice belonged to a man with a long brown face, a wide mouth that usually smiled and black hair cut short with a long braid at the back. The shoulder tabs of his grey tunic had gold circles

16

on them. He had once cheerfully told Dex that his hologram-tinted daughter drove all her boyfriends mad; Senior Controller Jahudi was not smiling now as Dex opened his eyes.

'You may well have contributed to the cause of the accident.' Even the sympathy sounded official in his quiet firm words. 'Marsbase has registered a very strong protest.'

'One of their people was bounced, too.' There was no sympathy in Romhilda's voice, official or otherwise. 'They're blaming you.'

'So this may be more than a demerit.' Jahudi's mouth tightened and he made to go. 'I'll do my best.' And if Friedelinde's very clever Daddy was uncertain, then Dex knew he was in for a bad time. Romhilda waited for an off-screen door to close before turning back.

'Console deck, one hour.' She made to disconnect. 'Oh, by the way Dexter, there's another old Earth expression: your ass is grass. Do you know what it means?'

It meant something very final, he knew that, because even Romhilda was sounding a little sympathetic now.

Day One of my bad time, thought Dex bitterly as next morning the Spoke link-shuttle – linker – docked at Cydonia, north-west Mars, with one very unwilling passenger. Himself. Friedelinde had been full of horrified dismay and Jahudi said it was the chance of a lifetime, hinting at double grades on return. Even Romhilda wished him good luck. Because sometimes people didn't come back from the dark side of the gas giants.

17

The linker airlock was a bubble set against the main installation. Once inside and the access door firmly shut behind him, a flat heavy smell of recycled air hit Dex's nose, mixing all the various odours of the base. The new electro-circuits in his boots made walking easier in zero gravity, but it was still a long sulky clump down the corridor. The boots were heavy and he was already tired and sticky; he wanted a bath, but even the hot water would be rationed here. And everything would be rationed even more tightly on the long-linker that would take him to Neptune.

Dex scowled and muttered something rude about the Martian colonists insisting that a Spoke cadet went on the flight. Replacing the fused tel-spark that relayed their signals to the planet, then repairing and activating the probe, was only a few days' work. But getting there – and back – was a long, long space-hike, even in deep sleep. A *year* of it and this time his mutter included Jahudi and Romhilda.

Two blue-skinned, blue-haired girls came out of a side-room, chattering happily and hands together. They saw him and broke off, their faces tightening into closed, hostile looks. He expected that and hoped there wouldn't be 'Tints' on the long-link flight. *And* he had to remember not to use colour nicknames down here.

'Hey, which way to Launch Dock, Seven?'

'A Spoke cadet on ground-base?' said one, opening her eyes wide with pretend astonishment. Her hair was in blue curls.

'Must be a hologram,' said the other. They were both taller than Dex. 'A real Spokie wouldn't get his hands dirty down here.' They kept going. There was nothing funny in the way they said Spokie or the look

18

they gave him. He even had to step back quickly to avoid being shouldered aside.

Dex scowled again and stopped to speak his request into the wall console. The on-screen graphic underlined the launch pad position on the base layout. Half a kilometre away and the moving floorway wasn't working, so it would be a long walk in his metal boots. This is going to be no fun at all, he thought, and hoped at least he would meet no more Tints on the way.

That chip on their shoulder about different skin colours seemed to be in their genes. Twenty minutes later he was at the launch pad waiting area.

It was enclosed, low-ceilinged and windowless. An air conditioner hummed loudly off-key and there was Rockie graffiti on the walls, most of it rude remarks about Spokies and 'Rainbows', the asteroid nickname for Earth people in general; Dex had never bothered to find out what it meant. There were only two people in the room. Both were Tints and both ignored him.

At least the man had an excuse. He was asleep, sprawled out over two chairs, a blue-skinned North-West Martian with long straight hair. His face was smooth-skinned and sharp-nosed with a tiny moustache like a blue pencil-mark. The woman was North-East Martian, green-skinned with long, dark-green hair gathered untidily at the back. She was seated at the table and bent over a tele-journal. Dex threw his bag into a chair and looked round the bleak, shabby room.

'This place is like a Rockie's moon boot.' He was hot, angry and his feet ached. 'Doesn't it ever get cleaned?'

'Is something not to your liking, Cadet?' The woman did look up this time. She had a sharp high-cheekboned face and blue-green eyes like laser chips.

Dex was hot and angry and his feet ached. And he was sick of stony-faced Martians who looked through him. 'I hope my bloody linker is cleaner.'

'And which linker would that be, Cadet?' The woman's voice was sharp as well and a little too polite.

'Neptune.' Much as he hated the idea of flying there, Dex couldn't resist swaggering a little. 'Special to tel-spark and patch up a probe.' Most Tints did only short-range hauls to the asteroids and Neptune was a gas giant. They only had token status on the longer flights.

'That sounds very important.' The man had woken up and was stretching himself lazily.

Dex was even more annoyed at the bland, mocking tone. A damn sight more important than Tints on a mineral hike, he almost said, then two things made him stop. The first was a closed glint in the woman's eyes and the second, a thin bar of gold on her brown overalls with the name CLEO black-lettered below. So he had to look at the man's overalls, faded from a colour once yellow and black-lettered with LAN. Then up to the flight board and the digital flight readout.

Neptune. Link Miranda.

Cleo and Lan. Even the cadets in their little Spoke-world circling Mars knew about these two, especially Cleo, and the fabled journey she had once made in Link Miranda. So Dex kept his tongue firmly behind closed lips and let the woman look him up and down as if he was a squashed bug. The man was smiling and his raised eyebrows invited Dex to go on speaking, knowing he wouldn't dare. Because Dex knew suddenly who was going to be the token on this flight.

Him.

'Waiting one more crew member,' said Cleo. 'We board when auto-charging is complete.' She bent over her tele-journal and the man closed his eyes again.

Dex was left standing there in the silence, knowing he looked as stupid as he felt. Then, behind, the door slid open and a young woman entered. She was brown-haired with a red-brown skin, dressed in a long blue shirt and slacks. She threw down her bag and looked at him hard.

'Are you Dexter?' Her words hurtled at him like chunks of space rock.

A Rockie from Ceres or Pallas, thought Dex, that was *all* he needed. Well, he out-ranked her so she could be put right in her place. 'Technical Electronics Cadet K Dexter, yes— '

That was as far as he got. The girl moved so fast that he almost didn't see her fist until it landed smack on his eye. She was punching two-handed and the second landed just as smack-hard on his jaw. Dex crashed back against Cleo's table and sideways on to the floor, taking a chair with him.

For the second time in two days, he lost consciousness.

3 Asa and Link Miranda

'What do you know about gas giants?' said Cleo.

Everything and you damn well know it, thought Dex, looking round. Cleo had cut her hair short in preparation for deep sleep and this was the first time he had been on the flight deck of a long-linker. It was quite narrow and shaped to a point; black space was only a metal skin and iron-glass thickness away. They had launched half an hour ago and Mars was a large red circle behind them. He was slow to answer Cleo's question and she went on calmly, as though teaching a kid to read.

'Jupiter, Saturn, Uranus, Neptune. A solid core of rock about the size of Earth. The rest is frozen gas and water held together with pressure. So we call them gas giants. Triton will be on your briefing disc. Any questions?'

Dex remembered not to make a smart answer. Cleo probably sharpened her teeth on cadets every morning and anyway she deserved respect. She had been flying long-linkers since she was his age. She had taken this one, Link Miranda, to Pluto and beyond, and been the first to actually sight the new planet of Stygnus beyond Pluto. Cleo had seen a new planet, unlike anyone else in the solar system, and had become the first person ever to stand upon its surface. She was a solar legend. And right now, those laser-blue eyes were glinting at him. He opened his mouth to answer, then remembered his jaw still ached and he would go into deep sleep with a beautiful black eye.

'Yeah, who hit me?'

'I did.'

The voice came from behind. Cleo had been about to answer, but shut her mouth and let her lips form a wry smile. Dex turned, making one hand into a fist, just in case.

The brown-haired girl was standing at the flight deck entrance. Now she had on the close-fitting blue and red-trimmed uniform of a flight cadet with the name ASA over the pocket. Her own hair was cut short and both hands were clenched into fists.

'But she won't do it again,' said Cleo calmly, looking at her console. 'Because you two will sort out your problems before deep sleep – understand?' A wave of her hand dismissed them.

Asa was already turning for the entrance again. Dex followed her through to the second deck where Lan sat. His long hair was also cut short and on-screen, he was plotting their course to the stop-over at Pallas, the asteroid base. 'Is our ship clean enough for you?' he said, grinning.

Asa spoke in that abrupt, quick way of hers. 'Lan, Cadet Dexter and I are going into the mess deck for a few minutes. Patch an energy unit through, please. Cleo's approved it.'

Lan shrugged and nodded and Asa kept walking in quick strides to the side mess room. It was long with two heavy portholes and a table in the centre. There were chairs on each side and over each, a virtual reality helmet, called a dream-cap. Asa rubbed a hand over her short hair and pointed at them.

'Choose,' she said.

'What are we fighting about?'

'I'll tell you under the dream-cap.' She pointed again. 'We've got the Roman arena, knights in a tournament, duel with swords and World War Two fighters.'

Dex wasn't going to argue any more. If the Rockie wanted a fight, she could have one. 'We've got much better choices on Spoke,' he said.

That annoyed her! 'We're not on your Spoke, we're on a Martian long-linker and you've got a choice of weapons!'

Dex made himself smile. Bad temper was never a good way to start a virtual reality fight and Asa's face was already flushing redder with temper. So he gave his best, 'I'm from Earth and you're just a Rockie,' grinned and sat down, letting Asa glare at him before replying.

'Rome?'

She sat down and flicked the operating switch on the dream-cap. The helmet-circuits hummed and the on light went to red as she pulled it down. Dex let her wait a moment longer, then pulled his own down. It ws time to teach this Rockie a lesson. The cool metal sides rested against his cheeks and the vision screen pressed over his eyes. He felt for the arm controls and the screen hummed into life, projecting him into a sudden hologram reality.

His dream-cap was linked to Asa so he 'saw' her in front at once, at least the gladiator image being linked into his own image-state. A woman gladiator – it would be – and clad in a short costume of leather and chain-mail. A helmet set with a snarling lion face-mask covered her face. Her figure held a trident

24

and net and Dex stepped back, adjusting himself. The net would tangle him, the trident would skewer him as he lay helpless and entangled.

Her voice buzzed in his ear. 'I've set the caps for a strike four bounce – OK?'

'OK.'

Thanks for telling me, he thought. Strike four would really rattle his brains if he let that net get too close. He was dressed in the same costume and could see Asa clearly through the vertical sunlit strips in his helmet. These dream-caps didn't have the sensor or even the smell-impulses of the newer Earth models, but they hurt just the same. He was holding a round shield and short sword and Dex knew he had the advantage – if he kept away from that net.

'Hey, Rainbow, want to know what we're fighting about now?'

'Yes!' he shouted into the vertical strips of yellow.

Asa's sandalled feet took a step back and she lowered her trident. Dex dropped his shield and quickly, too quickly, she sprang, the net twirling. Dex tried to duck back but the tangled folds, weighted with tiny lead pieces, wrapped round his body and jerked tight. His shield arm was trapped and his sword sent spinning away. Asa laughed, then she pulled again and he crashed to the hologram floor. The three sharp points of her trident flashed in front of his eyes.

'*Still* want to know?'

Dex lay there, rigid. He knew he was still in the chair and all this was just electronic graphics, but he would have to disconnect to get away; and Asa had set the chairs on a hard bounce that would just about knock his eyeballs together.

'Yes, if you don't mind.' He was furious with himself at the way she'd caught him off guard. This girl was very good and very quick.

'I was on the Mars control-link when that power surge happened.' *Now* Dex remembered the red-brown face scowling at him over a console. 'Me and Jona!'

Jona? The second girl.

'My friend!' The trident points nearly clanked against his helmet bars and he felt the tiny stabbing shock in his head. He lay still, not scared, but bewildered with a strange panic at the hate and rage in the girl's voice. 'We bounced too! I'm OK, but Jona went out. And she's still on Mars, though your Rainie friends were shipped back to Earth— '

'I never— '

'Shut up!' Her voice ground like broken iron. 'You Rainies think you can get away with anything. Well, you— '

A loud click flickered the tense bright computer image. The ground pressing him, the tight net and trident points disappeared and the helmet bars blinked into light. He was sitting rigid in his chair and opposite him sat Asa. Her face was a red-brown mask of tension and fury. Beside her, Lan took his hand from the disconnect.

'You didn't get clearance for that energy unit.' Lan's voice was mild but controlled, and strong like vulcanite made into alloys that even solar radiation could not penetrate.

'No,' said Asa. She didn't apologise and her defiant look challenged Lan.

'Don't do it again.' His voice stayed mild but Asa dropped her eyes and nodded. She headed for the door. Lan blinked his calm eyes at Dex. 'Who won?'

Asa turned. 'It's not over yet,' she snapped. 'You can take the unit out of my cabin batteries.'

'We want you in deep-sleep, not a block of ice,' said Lan.

'Cut her cosmetic power. I bet she never uses that.' Dex was still angry and humiliated.

Asa took a step towards him, her fist swinging. Lan put up an almost lazy hand and she stopped. She glared at Dex. 'Plenty of time to sort you out, Spokie.' She left.

Dex made to go, but the same lazy blue hand stopped him. Lan didn't speak for some moments, then he pointed out one of the big portholes at the disappearing red globe of Mars. Most of the features were hazy now, but they could see a broad sharp line down the side.

'Mariner Valley. Fracture line, about five thousand k's long.' The mild tone dared Dex to interrupt. 'On Earth, a hundred or so years ago, they thought it was a canal dug by an alien civilisation.'

'So?' Dex could still feel those trident points and swore that next time he would bounce Asa back to Marsbase.

'So things aren't always what they seem to Spokies,' Lan said. 'Asa not only saw her friend hurt, she was blamed and downgraded.'

'And she's hung up because I'm from Earth!'

Lan just raised his pale blue hand. There was a number and code stencilled across it. Dex shrugged awkwardly, the way most Earth people did when reminded of that. 'World Council outlawed those codes. It doesn't happen now. *She* hasn't got one.'

27

'She's got the skin colour, though. That doesn't go away in the second generation.' A stinging hard edge appeared in Lan's voice. 'She's an asteroid girl, she's from the Rocks, a Rockie. Like Cleo and I are Sandies. Tints.'

'Like I'm a Spokie or a Rainbow – whatever that means.'

'It means we are different!' Lan breathed heavily. 'This linker stops at Pallas for the last crew member. Asa and Jona have a lot of friends there.'

'Meaning?'

'Meaning you haven't got any, Cadet Dexter. So keep your mouth shut or you might lose some teeth. Now get ready for deep sleep.'

He left. Dex leaned against the porthole for a moment and watched Mars grow smaller. He could still see the shadow of the Mars Orbit passing over the red surface of the planet. He felt stupid now, and again had that funny little tingle of panic at meeting a lot of people just like Asa.

There might be nightmares waiting on Triton, but he had to get past Pallas first.

4 Cheese-riding on Pallas

The hard clank of the docking shuttle made Dex spill his coffee. 'No warning – thanks a lot, Cleo,' he muttered. He glimpsed a section of grey surface sliding past the porthole as the shuttle descended and another clank-clank as the airlock entry opened and shut. He began to unstrap himself. Pallas was the second biggest base after Ceres itself and base for the 'Jupies' who mined the outer asteroid belt and Jupiter's moons.

Dex's head still ached from the deep sleep. His hair had grown to shoulder-length and his fingernails were like claws. This trip was getting less and less attractive and even thinking up new names for Romhilda and Jahudi didn't help now.

'Pallasbase locked in,' came Cleo's voice.

He was eating a quick meal in the messdeck when the last crew member came in. He was red-brown like Asa with a big loose mop of dark red hair and a flat, tough face. The name REK was on his blue and red tunic.

'Hi.' To Dex's utter astonishment, Rek grinned warmly and held out a hand. 'Sorry Asa gave you a hard time.'

Dex stood, nodding, and mechanically took the hand. Rek's grin did not alter as his red-fingered vice suddenly crushed tight. 'Say hello on your knees, Spokie.'

'Nothing too rough, Rek. He's precious.' Asa had come into the messdeck behind him and went over to get coffee.

'Nothing rough – we're just saying hello, eh Spokie?' Rek's grin became more friendly and his grip more crushing. 'Kneeling.'

'OK,' gasped Dex.

He avoided the contempt in Asa's eyes. Rek's grip relaxed very slightly as Dex bent one knee. Then he straightened quickly, pivoting his hand to loosen the grip further. Rek swung his fist at once but Dex was turning inside the blow, slapping his other hand over. He locked his grip and Rek gasped as he felt himself thrown helplessly past.

'Far enough on my knees, Rockie?'

He was ready for Rek's reaction. It was as fast as Asa's his fist powering at Dex like a red-knuckled rocket. Dex stepped sideways, grabbed the wrist and used Rek's own body force to throw him flat against the wall. All the breath shot out in a long winded gasp and he sank down. Dex had his hand locked and pressured down. Rek gasped again, opening his mouth in soundless pain.

'Apologise for the bad manners, Rockie.' There was no answer and he pressed harder.

'You'll break his wrist first,' said Asa.

Her face was tight and sullen. She hated having to say that because it meant the Spokie had won. But she and Rek cracked their first asteroid together, and she knew how proud he was. She saw Dex give that unpleasant grin and longed to wipe it off his face, but Cleo had already warned her.

Dex stepped back, still grinning. 'Any time,' he said and left.

'Rek, I can fight my *own* battles,' she said. He just nodded, nursing his wrist. Cleo appeared in the door, her green-faced look scanning them both.

'Get on the coil with Lan. We're recharging.'

Rek went, still nursing his wrist. Cleo waited a moment, the flat heavy smell of recycled Pallas air stealing through the ship. Most of the base was underground and everything rationed even more tightly than on Mars.

'Asa, this is my first all-solar crew.'

'Dex— '

'Dex is a passenger. I had to be too nice to Earth-Control to get this crew together. To prove we can all crew long-linkers.'

'I understand,' muttered Asa. She did, too, and she was proud to be on Cleo's linker. But she still hated Dex and everything he stood for.

Cleo raised a green hand, the palm out, like a signal. The black code stood out clearly on her palm. 'So *we* don't want anything to happen to Dex, do *we*?'

She went over and poured herself a coffee. Asa breathed in that familiar air-smell and remembered there was a whole shift of miners in from Jupiter and the asteroids. Maybe Cleo didn't want anything to happen, but one foot out of line and Dex would wish he'd never left Spoke.

The baseroom was long and as low-ceilinged as those on Mars, part canteen, part gymnasium and part disco. One wall was lined with electronic games units, while dream-caps and graffiti crowded an art form of rude and happy expressions over the walls and ceilings. One side looked out through a thick bubble window on to the cratered grey surface of Pallas.

31

A huge hologram screen flashed on the end wall and the giant figures of a blues band jumped and danced to music throbbing loudly through dark red lighting. Red was reflected everywhere, on the tables, the window, even the people.

Asa sat at one of the tables, an untasted citrus drink in front of her. She was listening to the music, her eyes half-closed, thinking. Even in the year she was away, she knew she'd changed and the others sensed it, too. Rockies were tight and clannish and she'd been away among blue and green Martian Solies while they grubbed for minerals in the asteroid mines.

'A Rainie on Pallas,' muttered a solid, red-faced boy beside her.

He had the silver 'V' of a vulcanite probe-driver on his red tunic. Vulcanite, she thought, one more reason they don't like Dex. It's the miracle new metal of the solar system, indestructible, able to withstand meteor impact and also to be spun into transparent iron-glass; even the thinnest coating screened a hull against solar radiation. And coiled in an engine unit, bombarded with a proton drive, it took spaceships to undreamed-of speeds, letting Earth probe the very limits of the solar system. Vulcanite made Earth strong and kept the Solar Colonies weak. It was a symbol of their servitude, and so was Dex. He doesn't realise either, she thought – he's sitting there as though he owns the place. She tried to make herself forget him.

Dex sipped his soda. 'Don't they serve anything stronger here?' He had to shout to make himself heard over the pounding heartbeat of music.

'Yes, but you're not getting it,' Lan shouted back.

'Neither am I. Deep sleep and hangovers don't mix.'

Lan had appeared as Dex left Miranda. During recharging, nobody was allowed on board and when Dex headed for the canteen, Lan walked beside him without speaking. Dex knew he had a minder, but without admitting it he was relieved. In a base full of red-brown faces, he felt very alone and it was good to have another skin colour beside him, even if it was blue. He not only felt alone but very unliked; being on Pallas with genetically-tinted young miners was something he never dreamed would happen.

'Not impressed, are you?' Lan was smiling that lazy grin but his light blue eyes were cool and watchful.

'They're not all that impressed with me.'

Lan grinned again, but his eyes stayed cool. 'What did you expect, a red carpet?'

'Everything else is that colour.'

Dex shouted a little too loudly that time. A small group of the big teenagers at a near table turned to look at him. All wore the one-piece short-sleeved work suits of miners, all had the same look of Asa and Rek and an assortment of dark red and red-brown hairstyles – dreadlocks, close-cuts, long plaits and even mohawks. Asa was among them and more than once he had caught her closed frowning look.

Lan shrugged. There was just so much nurse-maiding he could do with this Earthkid. 'We like our colour now. It makes us different.'

'So why is it still a big number?' shouted Dex. 'So I'm the only one from Earth here and I had real parents and wasn't genetically made – so what?'

'Shut up!'

Too late. Lan cursed silently as the throbbing beat

33

of music suddenly stopped and the background noise slowly died away. The table group near them got up and came over. A big, broad-shouldered girl with chestnut hair in dreadlocks spoke first.

'Excuse me, Technical Electronics Cadet Dexter,' she said quietly. SELO was black-lettered on her tunic. 'My friend Hord has never met a real Rainbow with real parents and he'd like to say hello.'

'Hello,' said Hord. He was taller than Rek but had the same big grin as he held out his hand. 'Pleased to meet you.'

Dex caught the warning headshake from Lan and didn't put his hand out.

'What's the matter, Dexter?' said Selo pleasantly. 'Got a thing against Tints – or is it just Rockies you don't like?'

'That's enough— ' Lan made to get up but two of the big red-skinned miners were behind him. Each put a hand on Lan's shoulders. He strained a moment, then stayed there.

'Keep out of this, Sandie,' said one.

'I thought you didn't like nicknames,' said Dex.

'We don't like Rainbows using them,' said Hord. He still had his hand out. 'But most of all, we don't like bad manners.'

Dex got up and put out his hand. Hord gave it a tight pumping squeeze, very tight for just a moment, then let go with another grin. 'Not so bad, was it?'

'Yes, Rek, this Rainbow's nice,' said Selo over her shoulder.

Rek was standing back with another group. His expression did not change. Behind Dex, Asa stood up and came over. He didn't see that – or one of the big solid girls driving an elbow into her ribs. Asa collapsed into an empty chair and big red hands firmly grabbed her shoulders. The solid girl leaned over. 'Sit tight and keep out of it. This is for Jona.'

'Walk away, Dex,' shouted Lan. 'That's an order.'

'Yes, walk away, Earth-boy,' said Selo, stressing the 'boy' with another smile. 'This mining base is for Rockies. That's why they made us.'

'Walk away, Earth-boy. I'll even open the door for you,' said Hord.

Behind him, Asa struggled to rise and the solid girl leaned over her again. 'Want another elbow, Asa? We're only going to scare him.'

'Hey!' That was from Lan as two young women, their hair in pigtails, grabbed his arms and pulled him out of the chair. They dragged him over and threw him out of the canteen entrance, the door slid shut and Hord grinned again.

'Want to follow him?'

'Unless you'd like a little game of skill,' said the solid girl who had joined Selo. Her hair was tied in a casual pony-tail and her black-lettered name was BET. 'That's all right, isn't it Selo?'

'What sort of skill?' Dex knew he should have let them chuck him out of the door after Lan, but he had his own reasons for staying now.

Hord's grin was still full of strong white teeth. 'A joyride through the Cheese. You're a top Copy-capper – you can do it.'

'You don't have to.' Selo had exactly the same grin. 'We know that Earthkids break easily.' They were all grinning now, with all the warmth of solar

35

light glinting off crystal rocks. 'But Cheese never hurt anyone, did it?' Her eyes were wide and innocent.

'No.'

He was still trying to remember everything he'd heard about the Cheese as the grinning and ever-polite Jupies led him over to one of the big console chairs at the end of the canteen by the wall screen. They had found an asteroid, a big one about a hundred kilometres across and riddled with veins of the super-rare vulcanite. So piloted probes had burrowed through the asteroid, following the scattered mineral traces through and through until it looked like a giant version of one of those Earth Cheeses, full of holes.

'You both pilot a probe, get it?' Selo's eyes were still full of innocent fun. 'You each follow a mineral thread and first through is the best. Happy riding.' Dex was already in his chair and she clicked the controls to bring the helmet down over his head. Her big smile was the last thing he saw.

Then the helmet came on with a lightning hum. Hologram emptiness flickered and solidified into a scarred and pitted asteroid surface before him, riddled with giant holes as though someone had let off a monster shotgun. The same hologram reality had him enclosed in the narrow seat of a bullet-shaped craft, hovering before one of the holes.

'Ready?' crackled a familiar voice in his headphones.

Dex looked over. Another bullet-shaped probe was hovering beside his and the helmet enclosed Rek's red brown features. Rek must have ridden these things dozen of times, even through the real Cheese, and all at once Dex had the distinct feeling he'd been set up. There was something about Cheese-riding – it had been stopped for some reason.

'Ready,' he said. These little things *were* easy enough to fly and he *was* a top Copy-capper.

Selo's happy-sounding voice crackled a final time. 'By the way, Rainbow, the loser gets a bounce worse than Jona.'

'Go,' said Rek.

His own blunt-nosed craft was already moving as he spoke. Dex opened the control and shot forward into the same giant black hole. They would have the visuals patched through to the canteen's wall screen and already, he knew, shouting for Rek – Asa probably louder than any of them. Now the sides of the tunnel were closing round him and he made himself relax as both craft gathered speed. Asa was watching the wall screen but she wasn't shouting with the others. Her ribs still hurt and she was thinking hard, not about Dex but Cleo. But it was no use telling these miners that, she knew, because she was exactly like them. They wanted payback for Jona. The crowd round her were shouting now as the wall screen flickered with movement. It was split neatly into the 'eyes' of Dex and Rek and a graphic monitor kept score. Asa sat there with a hand over her ribs. Whatever Cleo had said, Dex was a cocky Earthkid and he had it coming.

Tense inside his hologram cockpit, Dex concentrated on the black tunnel ahead, ignoring Rek's own speeding probe beside him. Real probes moved slowly but there seemed no limit to how fast these ones went. He was gaining a little on Rek, but ahead the tunnel walls seemed to be closing in. Little side-tunnels were flashing past, too small for both craft to turn into. Then suddenly Rek's blunt nose jerked upward into another opening overhead. The tunnel sides kept closing and there were no more side-openings.

And Dex knew he was in serious trouble. He grabbed the control stick and tried to slow the probe down. But nothing happened; they must have locked the control stick on to remote and his fate lay in Selo's red hands. Already the speed was creeping up and the flashing sides became a blur. Then a jagged crystal spike appeared and he had just enough time to twitch the probe up and over. A scraping harsh edge of electronic noise told him he'd brushed the top of the tunnel.

'Hey!' he shouted.

'What's the matter, Rainbow, make a wrong turn?' came Selo's happy cold voice. He could almost hear the laughter behind it.

'This wasn't how we were playing it!' he shouted.

'We changed the rules without notice, the way Earth does!' Now Selo's voice was all cold. 'Enjoy the ride, Rainbow, and watch out for spikelets.' The intercom clicked off.

Spikelets! *Now* he remembered why joyriding had been stopped.

Inside the Cheese was crystallised lumps of vulcanite, too hard to cut so the probes had burrowed round them. But a probe moving this fast could not burrow; only his skill and instinct would keep him going now. So when one of them ripped its razor edges through the hologram metal skin of his probe, it would *happen*, just as the Rockies arranged it. And Dex knew this bounce would hit his brain like a sledge-hammer smashing moon dust.

'However you want to play it, Rockies!' he yelled, too scared to admit he was afraid.

He had wanted this confrontation. But now, with a clear creeping tingle of fear, Dex knew he had been too clever for himself.

5   Riding to nowhere

Another crystallised lump of vulcanite sprang up ahead like a solid set of crystal razors. He just managed to swerve the probe again and this time something scraped along the side. The tunnel was still narrowing as though he was being swallowed down a black speeding throat. Ahead another lump jutted sideways and Dex just managed to skid round it, so quickly that only instinct boosted his hands.

Now a wind-force was streaming down the tunnel and bucketing the probe. It hit the sides again, jarred sickeningly and sparks exploded in a shower overhead. Another spikelet shot into view. Instinct said upward and Dex jerked over another impossibly tight turn. Now sparks streamed on both sides as the tunnel became a closing stone tube. Selo's voice buzzed mockingly.

'Had enough?'

'Get stuffed!' That shot out too quick for Dex to stop it.

'After you, Rainbow.'

The probe bucketed again – the sides *couldn't* be closing more – then flashing into sight came the last spikelet nightmare, blocking the tunnel. Even as he tried to turn, the blunt nose of his probe was skidding against rock into those long crystal daggers. They were ripping at him, for he was too late to avoid them. Dex braced himself tight, waiting for that brain-crunching smash.

He lived a flooding black moment of utter horror. Then ahead the pointed crystal daggers seemed to be slowing down.

So was his probe, by long endless fractions of a second, until the sides of his fighter jarred again and, like an airlock shutting, everything went black. His wraparound helmet clicked with a small brain-tingling jolt and rose up from his face.

Dex blinked. Everything was dark and for a fearful moment he thought this was brain damage and he was lost in his own coma. Then lights came on around him. He was in the canteen and the Rockies were all silent. Beside him, Rek's dream cap had lifted and the big red-brown boy was stiff in his chair, looking ahead. He couldn't believe what he was seeing and when Dex looked, neither could he.

Asa had cut the power, stopping the game. Her hand was still on the disconnect and she looked round defiantly at the red-brown faces. 'Cleo needs him on the linker.'

'Who the hell cares what a Sandie wants?' shouted Selo angrily.

'He's on our crew. I can't let you do this.'

Selo took a step forward. 'Asa, he's only a Rainie and you are one of *us*!'

'I have to do what is best for the flight.' Asa's face was defiant but unhappy.

'You'll be painting yourself blue or green next,' sneered the solid girl, Bet. 'Then you can really fit in among your Martian friends!'

'Take the Rainie and get out,' said Selo, turning her back.

41

Asa flinched, but her lips were set tight. The music suddenly began again and she stood there as it pounded round her, ignored by everyone. Dex freed himself from the console chair, noticing the freeze-frame image as he did. The spikelet daggers of the tunnel were thrust out in all directions. That last obstacle would have been deadly.

Ahead of him, Asa turned and walked out. Nobody spoke or looked at her. They let Dex pass the same way with the loud hostile beat of the music pounding round them. Out in the corridor, Asa walked quickly ahead without turning around. Dex followed, Rek behind him.

'Thanks,' he said. She didn't turn or answer.

Cleo and Lan were coming the other way. Cleo took one look at Asa's face and let her pass. Then she waited for Dex and Rek to come up, blue eyes flashing like spikelet daggers. Even her voice was crystal and sharp-edged.

'We take off in one hour. Then I am going to sort both of you out – once and for all.'

The tone in her voice said it all. Dex found himself hoping the hour would pass slowly.

'Smartass.' Cleo said the word with a reflective sigh as though it explained a lot to her. She was seated at her control chair with the grey-pitted basketball of Pallas falling behind them, the base a twinkling metal dot in the centre. 'Well, Technical Electronics Cadet Dexter?'

Well, it means you accessed my personal life and read Romhilda's own sweet words, thought Dex, but this was no time for smart answers. In fact he had run right out of them. Cleo apparently didn't need an answer either because she whistled softly between her teeth for a moment, then went on. 'For example, a smartass is someone who makes a loud crack about colour and grandparents in a room full of gene kids. They never had even *parents*, so it hurts.' The blue eyes looked at him. 'Despite how they cover up.'

'Yes, Commander.'

'A smartass would know that was the best way to start a fight.' The console screen reflected her sharp face and those flashing eyes. 'Electronic or otherwise.'

Dex nearly repeated his response, but shut his mouth just in time. Cleo didn't need an answer – she knew them all.

'And if that smartass got a bit damaged, he'd be shipped back to the nice little orbit-heaven of Spoke instead of making the long hike to Neptune. Then an Earth-posting while the Tints on this linker waited on Pallas for someone else to program the tel-sparker. Right?'

Dex decided the best answer was not saying anything. That was *exactly* what he tried to do, even if nearly getting brain-scrambled was a little more than he bargained for. She had seen through him quicker than Romhilda and that was saying something. Cleo was still looking at her own green reflection in the console.

'Do you know why they cloned more women for the colonies than men?' Once again, she didn't wait for an answer. 'Because we are the child-bearing animal and therefore have a better body structure. And we're smarter, so it made good business sense.' Just for an instant, her voice sharpened to an edge of crystal hate. 'Asa is twice as smart as an Earthkid her age. Nearly as good as seeing through the juvenile tricks of a Rainie smartass as I am.' The last words flashed with a crystal bitterness. 'Confined to quarters. Get out.'

'Yes, Commander.' Dex had that really stupid feeling again. The same as when Romhilda finished with him. He turned to go.

'Cadet Dexter?'

Dex turned again. 'Yes, Commander?'

Cleo was still looking at her own reflection. 'I apologise for calling you Rainie. I don't allow racial slang on my linker.'

'Yes, Commander.'

Dex knew he was a long way from understanding Cleo. He went through to the second deck. Lan was sprawled in a chair, looking at the engine consoles. He yawned and smiled. 'Not even bleeding? Cleo must be in a good mood.'

'Restricted to quarters,' said Dex and kept moving. He needed a coffee and something to eat first and went into the mess deck. Asa was there, finishing a quick meal. She ignored him. He poured his coffee and punched a bean cake from the machine, but the silence continued.

'Thanks for disconnecting me.'

'Did you want it disconnected?'

Dex was about to make a sarcastic answer. Then he stopped. For the first time he realised he respected Asa now. 'Listen, I don't expect you to understand. But I was on Triton when it happened.'

'I've been under control-caps.' There was a distinct, Don't cry on my shoulder, Rainie, tone in her voice.

'And I saw my friends getting cut up and smashed to pieces.' Dex couldn't believe he was really saying this to Asa. 'OK, it was really Copies, but they felt it and so did I.'

'So did Jona.'

'I'm sorry about Jona.' And he couldn't believe that was the first time he'd actually said that to Asa. It was something he should have said the first time they met.

Asa's red-brown scan was as penetrating as Cleo's. 'What do you think happened on Triton?'

'I don't know.' Something else slipped past his lips, too quick to stop it. 'But I'm scared.'

Asa said nothing and he stood up, coffee in hand. This was the moment to grin, say something clever and walk out. He couldn't think of anything, so he just walked out as Cleo's impersonal voice crackled through the intercom.

'Prepare for deep sleep. One hour.'

Asa drank her coffee and decided against cutting her hair again. She threw the cup into the recycling unit and went down the passage after Dex. He hadn't closed the door to his cabin and looked startled at seeing her.

'On deep sleep, between Mars and here – did you dream?'

'I think so.' What the hell was she doing here – and why the hell was she asking him that? 'Anyway, I had – bad dreams.'

Asa walked just inside the door. 'You know how a Copy-cap controls android-remote? Well, your deep-sleep units do the same thing. They monitor brain rhythm the way sonics can map the surface of the planet.'

'And?' Dex had an uneasy feeling, though, that he shouldn't be asking Asa to continue.

'You can make a record of your dreams. That Triton experience must still be part of them.' She gave him a careful, secret look. 'Don't worry, it's safe.'

Dex was pulling off his boots. He would have to trim toenails *and* fingernails for this flight. 'Why the hell should I?'

'Because I heard before take-off from Mars that Jona didn't make it.' Asa heard her voice shake a little. 'So I want to know what happened!' Big tears were waiting to roll down her cheeks and she blinked them back angrily.

Dex kicked off his second boot. A month ago on Spoke he would have laughed, but now the gas giants lay ahead. And as much as he hated the thought of it, even a long space hike was better than brain damage. 'Set it up,' he said.

His door slid shut. Asa had gone without saying a word and Dex picked up his boot again. Just for the pleasure of throwing it at the wall.

'He'll do it,' said Asa. 'That Cheese-ride gave him a bigger shock than he'd care to admit.'

'And he's not so dumb, Asa.' Cleo was looking at her console readouts. 'He's programmed the deep-sleep unit on a lock key. You'll have to *ask* to see them.'

'He owes me a favour.' Asa's face was expressionless.

'So do I. You saved this mission today.' She stood up. 'Think you can mind the flight deck while I get my own deep-sleep unit ready?'

'Yes!' Asa grinned for the first time since she had come on board. Cleo grinned back, slapped her arm and left.

46

Asa slipped into the big black control chair. It was still warm with the closeness of Cleo's body and she put her hands over the console without touching the keys. For these moments *she* was in charge and Link Miranda would go where she wanted it to. Just as it had when Cleo took it to Stygnus.

The flight was as much a legend as Cleo herself and Asa loved to think about it. Martian pilots were restricted to short trips, but somehow Cleo managed the recharging and supplies and took off. Disobedience like that should have grounded her forever, but she had done something too special to overlook – set the deep-sleep units and taken her long-linker past Pluto to the estimated coordinates of the new planet. And she had found it, the way Earth voyagers crossed the unknown seas to find new continents.

Small pieces of the asteroid belt were still drifting slowly past, even though the new coil drive gave Miranda an awesome six hundred thousand kilometres an hour; but even at this speed there was a long, long journey ahead. Then they passed a larger asteroid, chopped into a half-eaten grey apple by mining probes. I love space, Asa thought. I love it because of the unknown and that beautiful sense of a black adventure stretched out in front of me. Perhaps that's how those explorers felt about their blue oceans. Soon it would be time to set her deep-sleep unit and the gas giants, Jupiter, Saturn and Uranus, would drift past unseen. By the time they got to Neptune, the sun would be a shining star, millions of black solar kilometres distant.

Thinking about deep sleep reminded her of something she had kept secret, even from Cleo. She had

47

inputted a monitor program through Dex's deep-sleep unit on the first flight without telling him and would have done so again if Cleo hadn't sent him so early to his cabin. She had already played that dream-tape from the Mars flight to Pallas. The visual pattern was patchy and distorted, but horrible images had flickered against the blue ice of Neptune's moon. She had dismissed them as nightmares.

Because nothing like that could be living on Triton.

6   Ice phantoms of the mind

Miranda was like all long-linkers. It was practically two smaller spaceships joined together, with a second control unit set in the rear and a huge cargo hold in the middle. Big as that was, it only just held the replacement tel-spark for Neptune. The solar-panelled gull wings touched both sides and were joined by a small streamlined vulcanite body and a drooped antennae beak.

Dex knelt beside the tel-spark, completing a circuit check. When the orbit settings were right, they would seal the hold, open the main bottom hatch and let the tel-spark take gentle wing in the black solar heavens between Neptune and Triton. They were nearly there now. His deep sleep headache was gone and he had cut his fingernails, toenails and hair again.

All Dex could remember of his dreams was that they were vivid and sometimes horrible. He was consciously trying not to think about it as he worked – or even about actually being so close to Triton. There were two giant portholes on either side of the hold and when he looked through the starboard pair, Dex would be able to see Triton ahead and Neptune behind it. So far he hadn't looked. He stood up and touched the giant gull-spread of wings. Finished. The tel-spark was ready.

'It looks like one of those wonderful Earth birds – albatrosses,' came Asa's voice behind him.

A few months ago Dexter's superior response would have been to ask what a Rockie would know about Earth birds. Now he turned, slinging the toolkit over his shoulder. 'There are no more albatrosses on Earth.'

'You could make them again from genes.'

Asa's tone was careful and smooth. She was inviting Dex to make a sarcastic remark about genetics and the solar colonies. He just shrugged. 'We've got to clean up the oceans first.'

He has changed a little, she thought. 'Cleo wants you.'

'As soon as the tel-spark's in place, we'll link your Copy signal and send you down.'

Dex could see Triton clearly enough now. It was blue-white with those pinky ice-caps and set behind it, the bigger blue-green bulk of Neptune itself, circled with two giant rings. Outside this, four of the smaller moons could be seen. He could see white specks on Neptune's surface – methane clouds on a hydrogen and methane atmosphere, thought Dex, and knew he was lucky not to be going there. Not even a Copy would keep its footing in wind-storms of eleven hundred kilometres an hour.

'Cadet Dexter?' came Cleo's cold voice again.

'Yes, Commander,' he said hastily.

'We'll have our co-ordinates in thirty minutes.' said Lan.

'I'll be ready,' he said.

Even Rek was on the flight deck for this briefing, so Dex wasn't giving anyone the pleasure of seeing how tense he was. He just nodded and went through to the mess deck. Rek and Lan clattered past on their way to the engine room. He took a squeeze bottle containing water and sipped it. His hand was shaking slightly and Dex put it on the table, angry with himself. Being scared, being too tense, might get him killed on Triton.

Dex sipped his water and watched through the mess deck porthole as Triton grew larger . . . twenty-seven hundred kilometres across, a density of silicate rock and water-ice, methane and nitrogen. Ice volcanoes of liquid nitrogen exploded sixty kilometres into the methane atmosphere. Triton had one distinction that Dex already knew about. It was the coldest moon in the solar system.

Who the hell does this Rainie think he was kidding on the flight deck, Asa thought to herself as she entered the mess deck. He's too tense and he's too scared to even tell us. This is outer space; we'd all understand, even Rek. We've all been through it. She poured herself a coffee and waited for Dex to speak.

'Here.' He took a small disc out of his tunic pocket.

'You've already looked?' she said.

He nodded. The computer had patched all the major sequences together. Asa hesitated a moment, then slipped the disc into the mess deck monitor. Dex looked at his watch. Eighteen minutes to go. The monitor screen flickered into a grainy broken life.

There were faces and movements, a row of dream-caps and the sudden whooshing blackness of the Cheese-ride. Then a girl's face frowning under red lights. Me, she thought, he's dreaming about me. Do I frown like that? Now the screen images were patching together in a clipped fast-forward pattern too quick to follow. Then suddenly it was clear and

51

phantoms were attacking at the monitor: a steel body and a sharp-pointed faceless thing; another thing with a smooth metal face and hideous empty eye sockets and the last – goggle-eyed, with a thick ribbed trunk where the nose should be. Asa recoiled – she had never seen anything so horrible. Then that grainy, patchy interference closed round.

Asa knew that Cleo had come into the mess deck behind them. Miranda must be programmed into its orbit pattern already. But even with Cleo there listening, she had to say something – show Dex she understood.

'Is that what you dreamed about?'

Dex nodded, then shrugged uneasily. 'Anyway, they're just dreams. They don't mean anything.'

'If something goes wrong on Triton, we'll get you back,' said Cleo from behind.

You'll try to get him back Cleo, thought Asa. But Romhilda is the best and she couldn't do it quickly enough. Something on Triton cut the signal and that something is still down there. And Dex knows it too, she thought. It was on his face as he looked at her and Cleo. He left and Cleo turned her crystal eyes on Asa.

'Asa, we have to do this. That cadet is the best Copy-capper on Spoke.'

'Those things— '

'*You* were in his dreams, too, and you weren't on Triton. I do know this solar system, Asa, and there's nothing alien on it.'

Asa nodded. 'But they looked horrible.'

'Just his subconscious. Now get the Copy unit ready.'

Asa went through to the next inset metal cabin. It

was like a mini version of the control room on Spoke, with two console units and a monitor screen. She began to program one of them. Overhead the lights went on and the sensor-gloves flexed themselves. She went through the preparations, thinking about those images she had seen. They were too like the first ones from the Mars-to-Pallas trip. And she felt scared, not only for herself but for Dex. Whatever Cleo said, whatever Dex tried to shut out, the coincidence was too real and too strong. No aliens in the solar system?

Perhaps not, but something was down there on Triton.

Dex was lying face-down in blackness. He was glued – no frozen – in a spread-eagled position, arms and legs outstretched, feet and hands digging into the solid ground. He could feel this and also how his mind was exploring the Copy circuits. And there was that little clickety sound as his brainwaves settled into them like an energy network. He was inside his Copy on Triton again.

Move your head, Dex, he said to himself. The all-over weight of the metal body held him down and he wondered how far under the ice his Copy would have sunk in a year. Something cracked along his metal back and he flinched. But it was ice cracking and the darkness was cracking, too, as he moved. Dex raised his head and through the vision strip saw the neat outline of his face in the ice below. He flexed his arms and moved his legs. More ice cracked. Stand, Copy, he thought. The metal android got to its knees then staggered and stood as the frozen circuits came slowly back to life.

'Do you copy?' crackled a voice in his ear.

'Yes, Commander.'

Dex breathed heavily and told himself – he had to *keep* telling himself – that he was back under a dream-cap and strapped into virtual reality sensory gear on the linker. His brain-waves joined them like a long invisible lifeline, one that could part more easily than wet tissue paper. Back on the linker, his hands were moving in the sensor-gloves, but on Triton his metal fingers were uncurling from their frozen grip. And when he told his brain to move his legs, one metal foot took an unsteady step forward. The ear circuits let the sound of ice splinter oddly in his ears. The vision strip cleared before his eyes.

'Try a few steps, Dexter. My hand is on the cut-off.'

Romhilda's hand had been on the cut-off too, thought Dex. He felt the tiny inside-creak of long cold interlocks as he turned the head back and forth. They would be watching everything he saw through the monitor. Lan would be propped lazily somewhere and Rek hoping Dex would put a metal foot wrong. Maybe Asa, too – Dex found himself hoping that Asa would be caring a little more.

'Have a look round,' came Cleo's voice.

Images of faceless metal things abruptly flooded into Dex's mind. He looked round too quickly and the interlocks creaked again. But the landscape round him, through his vision strip, was blue, cold and empty. It stretched away into pinkish highlands, the beginning of the icecap.

The interlocks crackled again as he craned his neck upwards at the black sky overhead. Up there, in the middle of the blackness, was the blue-green mass

54

of Neptune like a monster basketball, ringed with the dust particles that might be more destroyed moons. There were three of the smaller moons and moving through them was Link Miranda, just a tiny shining speck.

Dex was scared, but the magic of this standing moment never went away. He was up there in that shining speck, but his living awareness was standing down here on the surface of a moon where the real Dex could not survive for a moment.

'Anything?' Cleo spoke quickly, ready for him to interrupt, yell to disconnect.

'No.'

'The other Copies?'

'No.'

He had already seen their disjointed sections spread around and gently moulded in blue ice. A scatter of pink snowflakes began dusting over them as a wind blew from the polar cap. Nobody would ever get back into those Copies because they had been hacked to pieces. What could have done that, Dex wondered – and why didn't it happen to his Copy?

But he was back now and those horrors might still be out there, waiting.

'Check the immediate area. We've got you scanned – we'll see anything.'

You still may not get me back, thought Dex – Romhilda had us scanned and those things came out of nowhere. Dex shivered inside his metal body and began walking. His Copy legs were less stiff now and his arms were moving more easily. We really know how to build these things, he thought as his metal boots shuffled in the snow. Then his boot kicked something.

'What is it?' Cleo must be watching that scanner closely.

'Laser drill I think.' Dex knelt and began brushing pink snow off the object, breaking blue-ice fragments away as he wrenched it clear.

'Sure?' crackled Cleo's voice in his ear-circuits.

Dex knelt right over the object. He knew he was blocking the scan and he wanted to – because his vision strip and sensitive metal fingers were already telling him, disbelievingly, what he was uncovering. He blinked and something buzzed painfully through his ear-circuits like a power surge. He had to be careful, keep calm!

'Dexter?'

'Just checking, Commander.'

The words echoed strangely in his head. I am on Neptune's moon of Triton, Dex said to himself. This is the year 2044 and Earth is millions and millions of kilometres distant. And nothing from Earth but metal-skinned Copies have ever set foot on this moon.

'Hold it up and I'll get the image enhancer on it,' came Cleo's voice.

Dex thought quickly. He had to work this out for himself first, before this cold green-faced woman knew what he had found. So he stood and kicked blue-ice over it as he did. Another flurry of pink snow swirled round him.

'Just a broken laser drill.'

To his relief, Cleo seemed to accept that. The pink snow flurried again and Dex looked round. There was pink snow the last time the phantoms came. Goggle-eyed, pointed-faced, but no stranger than the thing he had just uncovered. He had seen something like it once before. His grandfather had shown him one when he was five years old. On Earth.

Dex could only dimly remember his grandfather, a very old man with a bald shiny head and long white hair on his chin that was called a 'beard'. Nobody had them these days. He had been to his grandfather's house only once and it was fantastic to remember it with an icy Triton wind blowing and pink snow dusting lightly over his bronze-skinned Copy body. His mind was wandering back to Earth and ten years ago . . .

'Dexter!' Cleo's voice buzzed sharply. 'Time to disconnect.'

Dex made himself think. He kicked more snow over the thing he had uncovered and looked up at the overhead linker dot, twinkling through the thick layers of methane atmosphere.

'One more circuit.'

'Be careful.' Cleo's voice sounded strangely different until he realised it was *Asa* speaking. Asa! Did she care enough to warn him?

Dex began walking. Grandfather . . . he was from a time when Earth cities were all above ground and not enclosed. Grandfather had lived in a big building with a lot of other people. He had held the thing in two shaking blue-veined hands; he had told the little Dex that *this* was a family treasure from his own grandfather, more than a hundred years ago when all the world was fighting; telling the little boy that one day it would be his.

But that hadn't happened. Dex trudged through the frost, in a wide circle, the pink snow falling more thickly round him. He had almost forgotten about the phantoms. Of course grandfather's treasure had not

57

come to him because pollutants, plague or radiation had sealed the city like too many others. And the thing that Dex's family ancestor used at a place called Somme was still there.

Now the pink snow was swirling thickly and some-where underneath it, he could hear that sonic signal that had come loudly screaming through Mars Orbit. Everything was swirling; he could hear Cleo speaking but his own voice could not answer because he was choking. Because the pink snow was too thick, wrap-ping thickly round him – something black-clicked in front of his eyes and the console helmet rose humming from his face.

He was looking at Asa and Cleo, Rek and Lan. He blinked and felt a little stabbing pain because that black-clicking moment had pulled his awareness up from Triton. All his disordered phantom thoughts still swirled round so vividly that their faces swirled round too.

'We were losing communication,' said Cleo qui-etly. 'Did you see something?'

'No.' He couldn't tell them that in the thick pink snow there were nightmares gathering. The sides of the console chair settled firmly round his body.

'No more double-images?' sneered Rek.

'You go down there— ' Dex nearly said Rockie, but bit it off.

'Enough!' Cleo raised a green hand. 'Sleep on it, Dexter.' And those cool blue-green eyes were scanning deeply and said Dex knew more than he was telling.

Dex went down the passage to his cabin. Triton was still so real that he could feel the frost crackling on metal skin. He sat on his bunk and tapped a research

58

code for Earth history into the cabin monitor. When it cleared for access, he punched in twenty requests and let them flicker across each other.

His monitor could be read anywhere in the ship, so he let all the different entries flicker across the screen again and again, until the one he was looking for leapt out in hologramic details from the screen; in outline, shape and detail, it was the thing that Grandfather had shown him.

A World War One infantry rifle and bayonet.

7 Things from the snow

'There's still time to program Rek into your Copy,' said Cleo.

My Copy would short-circuit on Rek's brain-waves, thought Dex, and nearly said it aloud. One sight of those phantom things and Rek would go from red to white. He just shook his head.

'No.'

Rek scowled and muttered something, but Dex lay back in the console chair and began setting the circuits. Lan's blue hands were moving over the co-ordinates. He turned and one blue eye closed in a lazy wink.

'You're ready,' said Cleo.

Asa was standing to one side. Some airlock doors away, in the cargo hold, was the long bronze pod in which her own bronze-skinned Copy would glide down through Triton's methane atmosphere to the surface. It would open and then, above, she would link her thought wave into the Copy and stand on the surface of Triton.

Asa knew very well that she was scared. Her lips were pressed together in a tight line and her stomach felt like a meteor was thudding round it. Dex was scared, too, she knew that, but he nodded for the helmet to be lowered. And he was looking straight at her as it did. Now she had to wait and it was like her first solo in a mining probe, or the first time she had gone through an airlock into outer space on her own – knowing she was scared and waiting to be terrified. Dex's helmet lights flashed with a little click that echoed in her own stomach.

The same black-clicking moment later, Dex opened his eyes through the frost-misted vision screen on Triton. He brought up one metal hand to rub the frost away. His old Copy had sunk into a cross-legged position since he had left it and, made from the indestructible vulcanite, it would sit like that until the end of time. Dex was already standing and turning round as he thought this. There was no more pink snow and all round him stretched blue ice and black sky overhead. But the snow would come, he knew that, and out of the snow, horrible nightmares.

This time he would be ready for them, but he had to move quickly.

'OK, clear.'

In only a few minutes he could see the bronze Copy pod overhead flashing against the frost-dazzle as it grew from a twinkling bronze thread to a long oval pod. It was controlled by Cleo's sure hand from the linker and skimmed down like a streamlined coffin.

'Can we send the pod faster?' Cleo's voice buzzed impatiently in his ear-circuits.

'No, atmosphere turbulence.' There wasn't, but Dex wanted to bring this Copy pod down as slowly as he could. The pod cushioned the Copy inside against damage on impact even if it broke open, but he wanted this pod intact. So he talked the descent carefully down and watched as the long oval pod slipped gently on to the surface, cushioning itself safely in blue ice.

Dex ran over as quickly as his metal legs would

let him and knelt stiffly. He slipped the catches with metal fingers; it was like opening a coffin. Inside lay the Copy, hands crossed over a bronze-coloured breast. Cleo was scanning closely and must have moved very quickly because at once the Copy vision screen blinked electronically and the bronze hands unclasped.

'Easy,' he heard his metallic voice say. 'You're all right.'

Asa's voice buzzed back into his ear-circuits, trying to hide a slightly scared and breathless note in her voice. So he made himself nod and because Copies could not smile, he raised a bronze thumb. 'Ready to begin repairs,' he relayed to Cleo and helped Asa's Copy to stand. They had to move fast!

They began setting up the probe again. Asa's electronic voice still buzzed slightly breathlessly in his ear-circuits as he looked round. 'I never thought I'd see Triton, a gas giant moon.' Just for a moment she sounded as happy as a child. 'Dex, we are more than four hundred thousand million kilometres from Mars!'

Yes, on a moon where nightmares happen, thought Dex. It was good listening to Asa, but there was too much invisible danger round them, watching. 'Stage one complete,' he relayed to Cleo and as he spoke, a faint scatter of something pink dusted on his bronze-coloured hand.

It was beginning to snow again.

'Weather's closing.' He forced himself to speak calmly as more pink snow dusted over his bronze arm. 'Cleo, I'm stopping work now.'

'We can go on for a while,' came Asa's voice. Her bronze Copy was kneeling, adjusting circuits. Just for

62

a moment it was outlined in pink snow and Dex felt a tingle of panic.

'I'm in charge – we're stopping!'

He hadn't meant to shout like that. Asa's Copy face looked at him and the silence in his ear-circuits said more than words. Now the snow was pattering round their bronze bodies and it was impossible to keep the tension from his voice.

'Ready, Cleo. Bring us up.'

'Check,' came Cleo's voice, then a buzzing click in his ear-circuits. That was supposed to be his Copy disengaging, but it didn't. Beside him Asa's Copy settled down like a cross-legged Bhudda because her thought power was no longer controlling it. But his was still alive because that was what he planned.

Dex looked round. The pink snow was swirling in gusts and he clicked off his ear-circuits because in moments Cleo would realise he wasn't coming up. She could check his Copy controls and find the missing circuits. Then she would be yelling at him while they were frantically replaced; but that gave him minutes and he needed time to see if the phantoms came again.

The pink snow was thicker and Dex kept turning his Copy round in a circle, telling himself this was stupid and wasn't going to work. Then instinct was *screaming* at him and Dex made his head duck. Only the movement saved him as a spiked ball brushed past his metal cheek. Dex sprang back on his bronze legs as out of the pink blizzard came a nightmare two-legged creature.

It was humanoid, metal-plated and with only a sharp, snout-like point where the face should be. It held a long pole with cruel spiked balls swinging on a chain; it moved in utter silence and very quickly. Dex ran quickly round the side of the probe, looking round for more, but it seemed to be alone. The creature followed, the sharp metal face looking at him.

The weapon jabbed viciously and swung again. Those spiked balls could smash his android circuits and the chains could entangle his legs. His ear-circuits buzzed again. Cleo must be frantic, but he had to make this work! So long as there was only one of them!

Now he was backing out into the snow again and the thing walked stiff-legged after him. Suddenly it broke into a shuffle and the spiked ball weapon swung in a smashing arc. Dex kept stepping back, looking round in the pink snow, lost for a moment – no, *there* it was! The open bronze pod that Asa's Copy had descended in. His bronze boot banged against the sides and he nearly tripped. But he was off-balance; the thing lunged at him again and Dex fell.

Now it was standing over him, raising the weapon. Dex felt his electronic circuits churn with fear as he rolled frantically sideways and kicked at the metal legs. It was like kicking rocks. He scrambled to his feet again. The metal creature was already jabbing forward again and then it swung viciously. Dex was waiting. He stepped inside the swing and his bronze Copy hands closed on the metal wrist. Here goes the first judo throw on Triton, he thought, then twisted hard, kicking the thing's steel-jointed legs from under it as he did.

It crashed forward across the pod, dropping the spiked weapon. Dex was still holding the metal wrist.

As it tried to rise he twisted again and it fell inside the pod. Dex kicked a steel foot inside, then slammed the lid and locked it. As he did, something else made of metal suddenly appeared in the pink snow over him.

Asa's Copy!

He clicked on the ear-circuits and her voice buzzed in an angry scream. 'What are you playing at?'

'In here!' Dex jabbed a bronze thumb at the pod. 'I got one of those things. Tell Cleo to send it up!'

'I heard.' Cleo must have restored the program that moment and the pod jarred and took off upward in a slow climb. Then her voice snapped again. 'Disconnecting.'

Dex took a step forward and grabbed Asa's bronze hands. 'Keep looking,' he yelled. They had to be on their guard because he could sense, not see, more of those humanoid metal things lurching out of the snow. Then the little black-click sounded and a spinning moment later the console helmet rose from his face. In front of him stood Cleo.

The look on her face made Dex wish he was back on Triton.

'You had better be right about this,' Cleo said.

She had listened in silence to his explanation and said nothing, even when he told her about the metal things that attacked him. Somehow her silence made the story sound stupid and unbelievable.

Now Lan had the pod on recall signal and was inputting an entry pattern into the main cargo hold. They were at the shuttle's main deck, on orbit between a giant blue-green semi-circle that was Neptune and the smaller blue moon of Triton.

'Coming in now,' said Lan.

'Get into your spacesuit, Dex.'

'Why?'

Cleo's laser blue eyes went cold. 'Because I told you to.'

The space suit lockers were in the mess deck. Dex was angry with himself as he opened one. Of course it made sense to open the pod as soon as it came on board. And to keep the hold an airless vacuum so that – if necessary – anything inside could be safely ejected. He knew why he was angry, too – because he was realising that being from Earth didn't matter outside Spoke. All these people were very good at what they did and he was the outsider. Asa entered and checked the voice-circuits on his helmet before he put it on.

'Thanks for coming back.' Dex didn't mean to sound flat and ungracious, but that was how it came out. 'How'd you talk Cleo into it?'

Asa gave him an annoyed look. 'Rek volunteered too.'

'Rek!'

'You really don't understand. In outer space, everyone looks after everyone else.'

'Even if you have to chase Rainbows?'

Asa didn't even smile as she slipped the helmet over. Her red-brown face was without expression as she sealed the clips. All right, it was a very weak joke, thought Dex, still angry with himself because he hated feeling this stupid. Even trapping that thing didn't seem clever now – or even real. His breath sounded loudly in the helmet as he clumped from the mess deck to the airlock leading to the main hold. The entry lights were glowing red because on

66

the other side the giant cargo hatches were opening into deep space.

'Enter now,' came Cleo's voice.

The door was still flashing red and a zap-zap computer voice said 'Airlock opening.' The two sides parted and Dex walked through. Asa stood looking at him, again without expression, as the door closed. Then the second set of airlock doors opened and he was in the hold.

'Get a jet-wire,' said Cleo.

Dex looked round. There was a row of them clipped beside the airlock doors, each a long coil of alloy wire and small jet, set with a handgrip, and he clipped it to his belt. Jet-wires were used when crew members went outside the linker; mooring line and propulsion in one.

'Ready.'

'No, you're not,' said Cleo.

Dex waited a puzzled moment and Lan's voice came on, lazy with amusement. 'It might be an idea to clip the wire to one of the wall brackets, Dex. We'd hate to lose you.'

His face was going red as he slipped the end catch into one of the wall brackets. There was nothing on the intercom and he knew – just *knew* – that they would all be grinning at such a dumb mistake. One press on the handle and he would have shot out into space when the hatch opened – and just kept on going into nothing.

'Are you ready now?' Cleo's voice had that sweet edge he didn't like.

'Yes, Commander.'

There were lights flashing red in the ceiling of the hold now as a section of black floor suddenly split in the middle, a black line becoming wider and wider as the two hatches slid aside. The floor of the hold could be opened as one giant hatch but Cleo was opening the smaller inset one. Now the black square of space was complete and the short blast of departing air ended. In the middle of the black square, still a long way off, was a gleaming bronze speck, twinkling itself upward through Triton's layers of methane atmosphere.

'Monitoring,' crackled Asa's voice.

The bronze dot grew into a tiny oval shape and behind it, Neptune's blue-green surface turned. Dex felt oddly calm now as though his nightmares were over. He had seen the thing on Triton, he had dared Cleo's anger and now he could show them all that his nightmares were real and coming into the linker.

The coffin rose into the black frame of the hatch under the remote control of Lan's gentle guiding hand. It turned in midair and came down to one side of the hatch.

'Go on, Dexter,' said Cleo.

The hatch remained open as he descended from the entry platform in his metal-soled boots. Dex knew they would all be watching on the monitor so he made himself walk alongside the edge of the open hatch with all of black space below, before he reached the bronze pod. He bent to slip the catches.

'Open it and stand well back.'

Dex did so. Then he balanced himself carefully and kicked the lid open, ready for that horrible pointed-face creature to come leaping out at him.

'Stand to one side. You're blocking the monitor,' said Cleo.

Dex moved to one side. He was shocked, empty

and dismayed. Nothing mattered any more and all that mad judo-scramble on Triton meant nothing. Because all he could see was a thin speckle of dust that rose and drifted over the black opening beside it.

The pod was empty.

8 Ghost creatures on-screen

Dex opened his eyes in the cabin darkness. He turned sideways on his bunk and flicked a switch. The cabin light came on and he sat up. He knew he'd only slept an hour or so, but that was all of the complete rest ordered by Cleo that he could manage. He pulled on his track suit and metal-soled boots.

He could still hear Cleo's cold, crystal-splintered voice. Nobody else saw that thing, she had said. 'You broke the first rule of space flight, Cadet Dexter, you disobeyed orders and nearly got yourself killed.' All of it delivered in tones of freezing contempt. 'And worse than that, Cadet Dexter, you put Asa in danger and she is worth ten of you.' Asa had tried to say something, but Cleo cut her short in that ice-grinding voice. 'Sleep period, Cadet, then we'll discuss it further.'

There was that same contempt in the eyes of Rek and Lan. Dex had broken one of the rules that held them together. More than ever, he felt out of place and somehow inferior to them all.

He was out in the passage now and walking towards the mess deck. There was nothing inside the pod but traces of silicate rock dust, Lan had said, adding in that lazy way, nothing that makes up to a monster. He went into the mess deck and over to the round porthole. Below, Triton turned up a bland blue face as though mocking him with its secrets. There was a snow-storm raging over the probe area now and it would be hours before they could go down again, even if Cleo let him. Because that thing, that monster, had vanished completely and nobody believed him.

'It did exist!' he said aloud through the porthole.

'So what happened?' said a voice behind.

Dex turned. Asa was sitting there against one of the consoles. The light from the screen reflected in soft shadows round her face and she flicked the console off as he came over.

'I don't know.'

'Cleo had your Copy on sonic even through the snow-storm. It was moving and fell over the pod – but there was nothing else there.' She was sitting on the console almost protectively, a hand covering the switch.

'You saw nothing?'

'I saw the closed pod, that's all.'

'It dropped its weapon. You must have seen that!'

'That pink snow was covering everything.' Her hand moved a little on the switch.

Dex stabbed a finger forward and the screen flicked on. Asa's teeth showed whitely for a moment and she slapped his hand from her own. Then she shrugged. 'All right, I put it on a graphic. So what?'

'So you did see it!'

'Something, that's all. I'm making this up from your description.'

She had made up a very realistic computer graphic, shining in hologram life on the curved screen – the long handle, the sharp spike on the end and those

71

cruel steel balls. Dex looked at it for a moment and then, without speaking, began to alter the picture.

'Three spiked balls, not two, and they were joined to the spearhead with chains. The spike was longer . . .' He was leaning over her to input and after a moment, she moved a little to one side. Dex sat down beside her. He could feel the stiff resisting pressure of her body.

'It looks like an old Earth weapon of some sort.' She put up a hand and flipped a brown plait off her shoulder. 'Even with cross-data, I couldn't relate to it too well.'

Dex finished his alterations to the picture. 'Try again.'

Asa shifted a little in her seat and Dex watched as her strong graceful hands moved over the console. The screen split down the middle, holding the spiked weapon on one side, dates and readouts flickering on the other. Asa took both hands from the keyboard and clenched them into puzzled fists.

'Impossible . . .' she breathed.

'Pole-arm, pike combined with ball and chain, general use from thirteenth to fourteenth centuries. Nicknamed holy water sprinkle?'

Asa grimaced. 'Some nickname,' she muttered. If those spiked balls hit someone properly they would sprinkle a lot more than water. And even asking how something like that ended up on Triton was futile. She leaned forward and began inputting more data.

Now a series of images flickered on-screen beside the spiked weapon. They were all humanoid, faceless and bizarre from the Earth world of six centuries ago. All were covered in close-fitting metal suits that Asa knew was called armour. People wore it to protect themselves in the days before gunpowder – fantastic steel costumes that were plain or studded, fluted in sharp lines or spikes, one looking like an android, another like an ugly iron insect shell; and the helmets, round, pointed, crested, metal faces made up as grinning masks or slitted into eye-holes and—

'That one!' Dex shouted and Asa's finger froze the image.

It was a close suit of plated armour with massive curved shoulders, huge elbows and knee-caps. The feet pointed into spikes, the gloves were long and steel and each finger was set with tiny spikes. But it was the helmet Dex remembered, a visor shaping forward into a sharp point with tiny breathing holes on either side and those slitted eye-holes.

'That type of helmet was called a pig-face.' Asa was reading softly from the screen data, aware that Dex was shuddering very faintly beside her, reliving the nightmare. 'Shaped into a sharp point to deflect blows.' She unclenched both her hands and raised them to her own face, as though demonstrating. But she knew she was practically in the same state of shock as Dex. The screen data said mid-fourteenth to mid-fifteenth century. And that was impossible.

She rose to get them both a coffee. She wanted to take Dex's hand and tell him there was an explanation for all this, there was *always* an explanation. But there wasn't and the Earth-boy didn't need futile remarks right now. She put the coffee down beside him and gently pushed his hands towards it.

'Thanks,' muttered Dex. He only took one sip then cleared the screen and began inputting another shape.

'Is that one of those old . . . rifle things?' said Asa uncertainly. The crystal laser had made them history just as gunpowder did to armour.

'World War One infantry rifle and bayonet, 1903 Springfield,' said Dex softly. 'I saw one like it on Triton.' He set his lips tightly against Asa's curious look for a moment. 'If I'd thought to cross-match it like you did with the pole-arm, then – then I wouldn't have put you in danger. Sorry.' He made his tight lips smile.

'A Rainie apologising, do my Rockie ears receive correctly?' Asa smiled back but it quickly went as she looked at the screen. '*That* thing attacked you?'

Her voice reflected his own disbelief, Dex thought, perhaps his own chill of horror, too. All the brief glimpses of that thing were on-screen. The goggle eyes that were flat round discs of glass set in a rubber mask, the 'snout' that was a long rubber tube down into a breastpack.

'World War One American infantryman in gas-mask,' he recited from the data. 'They were called dough-boys.' Now Dex could feel a force field of unreal horror round his body, like tiny frozen needles jabbing painfully all over him. A World War One foot-soldier and an armoured medieval knight. He closed his eyes. This was worse than a nightmare.

'Nightmare . . .' said Asa, unconsciously echoing his words.

Dex nodded. 'Have you told Cleo anything?'

'As it happens, no.'

The cool voice came from behind them. More of the mess deck lights came on and Cleo entered. Rek

74

was behind her at the door and gave an unpleasant grin.

'I patched your ghosts through to the engine room console,' he said.

'All right Rek,' said Cleo in a go-back-to-the-engine-room tone of voice. He turned and left and Cleo came over. Dex silently ran the program through the console again but Cleo just stood there, her lips pursed, her face closed of emotion.

'That's it?' There was cool disbelief in her voice and even cooler sarcasm. 'Problem solved. Dex was attacked by a knight in armour and his friends bounced by trench soldiers from last century.'

'I saw those things.'

'No Cadet, you *think* you did. Finish your sleep period.'

Dex stood up and pointed at the screen. 'Am I supposed to have made all this up?' he shouted.

'You tell me.' Cleo's voice cut like a laser saw. 'Guilt-related? Made up in your subconscious to cover what really happened to your friends?'

'Yes, what did happen?' shouted Dex again.

'They were bounced because you disobeyed orders. The way Asa was put in danger!'

'No!' Dex was feeling his face go white now as that nightmare sensation began prickling all over his body again.

'Then how did two things from Earth history appear on the surface of Triton?' Her laser sharp voice snapped in disbelief – and dislike.

Dex opened his mouth to try. Then quite suddenly he realised that he couldn't because she didn't *want* to believe him. Lan had come in and was silently watching him. Dex looked at Asa but she was silent too, seeming a little more tight and embarrassed. Then he turned and left.

'That wasn't fair,' Asa heard herself saying.

'Remember Jona.' Cleo's laser sharp voice cut viciously.

'I haven't forgotten Jona!' And that was her own voice screaming because the memories were still too painful. She saw over the console and heard Cleo's booted footsteps come over. A hand came on her shoulder, sympathetically tight.

'We all care about Jona. But that doesn't concern Dex. Not now.'

Asa opened her eyes and looked up. 'I don't understand.'

'It's very simple.' Cleo's voice was sympathetic, too, but firm with resolution. 'Dex *has* to think he is imagining all this. That it *is* all in his mind.'

Lan's voice always sounded lazy. 'Because there *is* something down there, Asa. Something we don't know anything about.'

Asa looked at them both.

'Something alien,' said Cleo.

9 Something out of Triton

Lan took a disc from his tunic pocket and held it up questioningly. Cleo nodded and he went over to slip it into the monitor. Cleo squeezed Asa's shoulder again. 'Top secret Asa. To us.'

That 'us' was already beginning to answer questions for Asa. That tone of voice, the word said in such a complete and assertive way. 'Us', the solar colonists in the quadrants of Mars and through the mining stations of the asteroid belt. The blue, green and red people who were made for outer space, human beings with no links to Earth except their unknown gene source. And even that was strange because they had been genetically tinted to keep them separate.

'Dex found something on the surface of Triton when he went down the first time,' said Lan.

'A broken laser drill,' said Asa.

Cleo smiled tightly. 'Which he was careful to cover from our scanners and spent a lot of time kicking snow over. We plotted the co-ordinates and Lan went down in a Copy.'

'Only this time I patched the Copy's visuals directly to our scanners,' said Lan.

Now, on-screen, she could see bronze hands digging into the blue frost. Ordinary human hands would have torn themselves apart before they cracked that frozen surface. Now the Copy hands were pulling something out, cracking the blue ice from it. They ran down the long barrel, clearing it of ice and even working the mechanism at the end. Asa could almost hear the trigger click as it was pulled.

'World War One rifle in full working order', said Lan calmly.

'Real . . .?' whispered Asa.

'Not in minus 400°C.' On-screen, Lan's bronze fingers were running over the controls, even feeling along the sharp edge of the bayonet. 'A perfect duplicate, but the real things were made out of wood and steel. This is an alloy of some sort, all over.'

'What about that thing in the pod – how could it vanish?'

'Watch,' said Cleo.

On-screen, one moment Lan's bronze-fingers were handling the rifle. Then a tiny scatter of pink snow came over and it suddenly vanished in a sharp twinkle of light. 'Whoever made that somehow realised we'd found it. So I got away quickly.' Lan's grin had an edge of tension in it. More pink snow was misting over the screen before it cut to black. As it did, Rek's voice sounded on the intercom.

'I'm scanning a force eight disturbance on Triton, by the probe co-ordinates.'

'An extra big ice volcano blowing its stack, Rek?'

'Not sure, Commander. Not the pattern for one, and since it's right by the probe— '

'All right, coming,' interrupted Lan and cut the intercom. He looked at Cleo. 'Anything happening on Triton right now should interest us.' She nodded and he left.

'Why don't you want Dex to know the truth?'

'Because he doesn't matter.' Cleo took the disc

78

from the monitor and zipped it into her pocket. 'Asa, you know about the terraforming plans on Mars. And you know Earth is still blocking them.' Her voice was soft as melting steel. 'Do you know why?'

'They want to go on pulling our strings.'

'Yes. They do.' Cleo's smile was like steel too. 'And terraforming means we will need more of the resources we mine for them. More say in what happens. And Earth is too greedy and selfish to let that happen.'

'So we have to find new resources.'

'Yes. And keep everything we find secret. Otherwise Earth will send in an army of androids.' She pointed through the porthole at Triton. 'And not just minerals, Asa. Whatever is down there on Triton belongs to *us*.' Her voice was as cold as her blue-green eyes now. 'The people of the solar system.'

No, Dex can't matter, thought Asa. He's caught in the middle of another Earth-Mars power struggle; his own people would do the same to her. And he would have to live his nightmares alone because Cleo's 'us' meant her as well.

'Us,' she said.

'I don't know what that thing down there is,' said Cleo. 'But knowledge is power. And we *need* power for Mars to be a real planet.' She paused, then added softly, the steel gone from her voice, 'For everyone.'

'Cleo.' Lan's voice came urgently on the intercom. 'That disturbance level is building. You can get a visual from the rear observation or shall I patch the scanners through?'

'I'll join you.' She was already heading for the

door. 'Asa, patch Control through to the rear. We'll finish this later.'

'Yes, Commander.'

Cleo made to say something else, then left. Asa walked quickly to the flight deck but there was none of that little thrill of command as she slipped into the big black Control chair. She was still thinking about Dex and still feeling sorry for him. What the hell was happening to her?

Patching Control through to the rear only took a moment. Cleo's terse voice acknowledged, then Asa bought Triton up on the forward scanner. Beyond lay a section of Neptune and a part of the broad flat rings. She focused the scanner picture more closely to the pink ice-cap. Just to one side of it, a circle of gleaming flashing light had formed. Cleo's voice came again, very tight.

'Asa, stay in forward control, helmets on, tell Dex.'

'What is that thing?' There was a helmet locker under the seat and she was already reaching for it.

'Forcefield of some sort. We may go out of orbit.'

It was a very strange forcefield, thought Asa. Now the gleaming circle seemed to be unpeeling itself like taking the skin from an Earth orange. She'd only ever unpeeled one orange – a very special treat for a ten-year-old Pallas girl. What was she thinking about that for? Asa shook her head angrily and slipped the helmet on, click-snapping it into place. Then she pressed the intercom.

'Dex, put your helmet on.'

On the scanner now, the ring seemed to have uncoiled itself and was floating lazily up like a strip of tinfoil. 'Just a freak energy emission I think,' came Cleo's voice, 'but I'm taking Miranda into a wider orbit.'

The linker shuddered as she spoke and Asa's view of Triton slid out of the scanners as Miranda turned. Asa felt a sudden little tingle of alarm as she adjusted the scanners to bring Triton back on-screen. That tinfoil strip seemed almost to alter course with the linker. The tingle of alarm came again and she realised Dex hadn't answered.

'Dex, respond,' she said, flashing his cabin circuit again.

There was still no answer. Oh, you stupid Rainbow, you've caused enough problems, she thought. If Dex had his intercom off then he only had himself to blame. He was supposed to be in his cabin, not wandering somewhere on the linker. And if an emergency was coming, she had to stay here in forward control. *And* while she was telling herself this, Asa was running as fast as her heavy boots let her, down the passage to the crew quarters. The feeling of something bad was flowing through her like cold water. She hit the button to open Dex's door.

His cabin was empty.

Through his porthole now, she glimpsed the surface of Triton again as Cleo took the linker hard away. Now that thin tinfoil strip was floating through the upper layers of atmosphere. It was like nothing she'd ever seen before and the bad feeling was flowing more coldly in her body. Dex's helmet was on his bunk; she grabbed it and ran clumsily out. The mess deck was empty. She ran towards the cargo hold.

That cold feeling was churning away in her stomach now. It seemed to make her body rigid, slow down her booted feet and make a thick lump in her throat.

Her hand pushed the first button and Asa stepped through the opening airlock. Now her boots almost floated slowly and her breath misted the helmet visor and she clicked it up without thinking, pressing the second button hard. As the doors slid open, Cleo's voice buzzed in her helmet, sharp with alarm.

'Closing airlock doors. All crew strap in.'

The second airlock doors stopped opening and began to close again. Asa threw herself through as they thudded shut behind her and Miranda shuddered more strongly. We're going to full power she thought, emergency! Then she saw Dex.

He was in his space suit, standing by the open pod. He must have heard Cleo on the linker intercom that time, but he was open-mouthed with disbelief because that tinfoil strip had suddenly zoomed as high as Miranda. Now it was joining itself end to end and cartwheeling towards them, flashing like a golden chainsaw blade. Asa realised the thing was huge.

'Dex!'

She threw the helmet. It tumbled slowly through the air and Dex turned, unfreezing from his trance. That unreal sense of slow-motion horror possessed Asa again as Dex reached out his hands to grab the helmet. And outside, through the porthole, the golden saw was whizzing towards them with impossible speed. Cleo's voice screamed through the intercom.

'Crash stations!'

Dex was fitting the helmet on his head and clumping over to grab a wall bracket. He slammed the helmet down and Asa suddenly realised she shouldn't be able to hear it seal. Her own hands flew to her visor and slammed it down. And there was something else she should have done. She was turning to do that, to grab for a wall bracket like Dex, when the golden saw cut into the side of Link Miranda.

There wasn't even a jar of impact – just a sudden blaze of golden light, dazzling and blinding Asa through her helmet as she grabbed for the bracket. She missed and a screaming intense hum of energy blasted round her. She made another grab but the force sucked her away and upward. She should have slammed against the ceiling of the hold, but it wasn't there any more and Asa felt herself going further upward.

Terror and a horrible sense of unreal nightmare seized Asa. Because she was *above* the linker now, because that golden saw had sliced through Miranda like a knife through a cake. Bow and stern fell away in two halves below Asa and the blast of departing air threw her even further into black space.

10 Crash dive

The same blast of departing air struck Dex, but he was already gripping the sides of the cargo hold. The golden light dazzled painfully, beating sun-strength on his helmet and he glimpsed the saw spinning away into the blackness. Now the stern end of Miranda was falling away, the sides sliced as neatly as scissors through paper. And with a worse sense of nightmare, he saw Asa's space-suited body tumble overhead as the outdraft sucked her into space.

Cleo's end of the linker was spinning and helpless. And the blast of air that threw Asa out would keep her tumbling forever in the blackness. Already she was distant and Dex grabbed a jet-wire, locking it to the bracket and pressing the button.

'Asa, I'm coming,' he yelled in case her intercom was still working and he held on to the jet-wire with both hands, letting it pull him into space. The silver wire uncoiled behind.

In the same fraction of a second, three questions slotted themselves into Dex's mind – whether he could go fast enough, how much line he had, and how long it would be before the bows of Miranda jerked him back like a fish on a hook. Asa was ahead, still too distant, and he pressed the button harder, not daring to look behind at the unrolling wire. He was going at full speed now and waited with a sick dismay for it to jerk tight. Was Asa closer?

Dex felt sick, mad, shouting crazily into his dead intercom. 'Asa, I'm coming – coming!'

The two halves of the linker were still falling back but the stern section had stopped spinning and seemed to be coming under control. Then from the rear end of the airlock, a bronze pod shot out and headed straight for them. Cleo had ejected an empty Copy pod at full power towards them like a speeding lifebelt. It was desperate, but the only thing she could do as she struggled to regain power. As it headed towards them, the jet-wire he was holding wrenched, nearly tearing loose from his hands as it stopped.

Asa was still helplessly ahead. But she had seen the pod and reached towards it, hands and legs wide as it skimmed towards them like an oval surfboard. As it passed, she grabbed with both hands, but they slid down the smooth sides. Dex yelled again into his dead intercom as the jet-wire began dragging him back. Then Asa's hands locked on a raised end of lid and she hung on.

Dex was being pulled back, but Asa's pod was coming towards him, all without a sound except his own voice yelling with futile anger. The pod whizzed up, and he let go of the jet-wire with one hand. Asa grabbed with hers as the pod skimmed by and their gloved fingers locked. His other hand was nearly torn from the jet-wire handle, but they held each other tight and Asa was being pulled back after him.

'Hang on, hang on, hang on!' he kept shouting into the intercom. The surface light from Triton was dazzling on Asa's helmet and he couldn't see her face, but had an odd sense she was grinning. Maybe being lost in space wasn't as traumatic for a girl born in space. She was pointing forward and he remembered to reverse the jet-wire and take them back faster to the linker, the wire falling in a long loop behind. Their stern end of Miranda was almost out of sight now, but ahead the bow section grew larger.

There was another problem, though. Already the bows were beginning to dip towards Triton, no longer under control. Asa jabbed her free hand ahead and then pointed at herself. Let me take us in, it said, and Dex nodded.

Dex saw Asa touch her gloved hand over the cut sides of Miranda as they went past. Something of incredible sharpness and force had sheared them smooth as glass. She reached out to grab a bracket, then the stairway ladder and Dex grabbed it behind her. They were almost upright now because the linker was still diving and below, Triton was closer. Ahead of him, Asa punched the manual controls of the first airlock door and pulled him in after her. The airlock slid shut; she punched open the second and they stumbled through. The second lock closed.

Asa was still pulling him along. Miranda was on a death-dive and there was no time to lose. They stumbled across deck and walls, even the ceiling, as the bows tumbled. Asa grabbed both sides of the entrance and forced herself into the flight deck. Dex followed, shutting the door behind him. It locked tight and he tested the air pressure to make sure they could breathe outside their helmets.

Asa was already in the control chair, strapping herself in. The blue-white mass of Triton was filling the observation windows and there was no time to lose. He gestured to her helmet, raising his own as he did. 'Asa, you are the most incredible young woman in the solar system,' he said as her helmet visor snapped open. She was already yelling into the intercom.

'Cleo, this is Asa, bow section. Can you receive us?'

Her face was pale under the red-brown skin and she was breathing quickly in little gasps. For the last endless minutes she'd been fighting against burial in a black solar grave. Dex put out his hand, but she just raised her own – she was OK, it said.

'Cleo, are you receiving?'

Another long silence, then Cleo's voice from far away. 'Asa?'

'Yes. Dex got me back.'

Cleo's voice came back, choked and a little stronger as though the ship's power was restoring itself. 'Good .. oh good.' Another silence, then she gasped a little as she went on. 'Can you make another orbit, we can meet –' Her voice was lost in a splutter of static. Asa guessed Miranda's other section was so far out it would have to go round Neptune first.

'No, we're inside yours, headed for the surface.'

'Listen carefully.' The distant voice spluttered again and Dex felt the flight deck steepen underfoot. 'A linker can be controlled fore and aft in case the bows are damaged, you know this. So we can still manoeuvre the stern and send a life pod down. You have tanks of air, food and water and your computers are on sealed circuits. There is a program for descent and retro-rockets – do you copy?'

'Copy,' said Asa.

The static spluttered again. 'I'm sending you co-ordinates, voice-ac them to the guidance system.'

'Understood,' said Asa.

'Tell Dex he did well. Stand by for co-ordinates.'

Asa gave Dex a grim little smile. She waited as the instructions came through, then repeated them in a clear, steady voice into the console. An acknowledgement zapped back and Miranda's bow section shuddered as the rockets fired and oncoming Triton steadied itself outside the windows. Asa sighed.

'On course.' She paused a moment. 'Cleo's locked us to the probe site. It's her only plotted co-ordinate.'

'Is that safe?'

'Is anywhere on Triton safe?' Asa shrugged. 'We stay in the bows and wait for the life pod.'

Cleo's voice came again, almost lost in the static. 'Bow section, we're nearly out of range. Sit tight, you're safe and I'll get you out, repeat, I'll get . . .'

Her voice faded away. Now the blue-white of Triton was filling the forward observation window completely, with just a curved black edge in one corner. The bow section jarred a little as it entered the atmosphere and they jerked in their seats against the tight straps. Asa abruptly held out her hand.

'Thanks.'

'You saved me first.'

'Yes, and what the hell were you doing in the hold anyway?'

'Checking that pod – I couldn't sleep— ' Dex broke off. 'I was looking for answers, Asa. I didn't make all that up.'

'I'm not saying you did.'

In fact I know you didn't, but I can't tell you, said Asa to herself. The bow section jarred again and the blue-white surface was closer now. An edge of pink ice-cap was showing. And this is an

unreal conversation to be having at fifty thousand
k's an hour, going through a methane atmosphere.
Something else came to her, nearly as crazy.

'Listen, does Friedelinde know?'

'Friedelinde!' Dex shot a startled look at her.

'Sure.' Asa was breathless, pressed back in her
chair and hands gripping the rests. 'We monitor all
those post-sparks at Marsbase. We get a big laugh
out of Friedelinde-with-the-ever-changing-hair.

Dex looked at her suspiciously. 'And what's she
supposed to know?'

The bow section thudded and Asa's grin was more
strained. 'That I'm the most incredible young woman
in the solar system?'

She had heard. Dex looked at her, then suddenly
the ice surface was rushing past and the rockets
fired, lifting the nose up. Another kicking thud
ran through the bow section and a thick flurry of
ice-blue frosting rose on either side as Link Miranda
slammed down hard and skidded over the smooth ice.
A hard clank and slowing jar came from behind as
the big parachute opened to slow their rushing speed.
Miranda thudded again and lurched a little sideways,
slamming itself to a stop in a thick cloud of ice. It
settled and a line of snow appeared at the bottom of
the observation window where the bow section had
buried its nose. Then there was silence.

'We're down,' said Asa unnecessarily.

'Feels like it,' muttered Dex. He should have been
feeling relieved, but all he could think about was that
gooey spark he'd sent Friedelinde on her birthday.
Everyone at Mars base must have read it.

Asa was trying to raise Miranda's stern section
again. 'They must be way over on the other side of

Neptune by now,' she said. 'I'll set a homing beacon so they can track us.'

'Then we go home in half a linker?'

'It sounds crazy, Dex, but we can.'

'And what do you think cut us in half?'

It was almost the first time they had remembered it, as though what happened was so impossible that they had pushed it from their minds.

'Something from Triton – a forcefield? It came from under the ice-cap.'

'We're just about *on* the ice-cap,' muttered Dex. Outside, the blue snow was merging into a line of pink highlands. 'I know you don't believe me, but that thing came out of pink snow, I'm sure it did.'

I believe you. Asa's lips nearly formed the words, but that fierce 'us' of Cleo bit into her mind. 'If anything attacks, we're safe in here. It would take an army to get in.'

'That soldier might have been part of an army,' said Dex grimly. 'Are there any guns on board?'

'You know the rules about guns.' Rules of course that only applied to the solar colonies, thought Asa, but she didn't want to start a fight right now.

'I'll just check through the ports.'

'I'll come with you,' said Asa, unstrapping herself. If Dex was crazy enough to launch himself into space on a jet wire then he was crazy enough to go outside. Dex nodded. At least he knows I'm in command, she thought, and led the way to the airlock.

They sealed their helmets and checked intercoms before going through to the second airlock. The inset iron-glass window showed nothing but frozen pink and blue desolation. A deep score mark stretched behind them and just outside lay the tangled mass

90

of the alloy cord and mesh fabric of the braking parachute.

'It's not snowing,' muttered Dex. Asa looked at him. 'Those things came out of the snow for some reason.' His voice crackled desperately through her intercom. 'Asa, I have to know I'm not mad.'

'You're not mad, Dex.' But he was mad enough to come after her into deep space and she could still remember her terrible panic before his hand grabbed hers. And still without quite knowing why, she said 'Let's just go out on the landing platform, OK?'

Dex nodded and grinned his thanks through the helmet visor. He's got a nice grin, thought Asa, and smiled back. She's got a nice smile, thought Dex as the door opened and they cautiously stepped out on to the landing platform. Once it had led down into the hold, but now the broken metal staircase ended abruptly in a frozen mass of pink and blue. Overhead was a black sky and the huge blue-green ringed mass of Neptune. Another two moons were in sight and, somewhere behind it all, Cleo's half of Link Miranda would be limping long black hours round the planet before coming overhead again.

'Nothing,' said Asa through the intercom.

'We should check for hull damage,' said Dex.

You just want to flush one of those things out, thought Asa. I'll decide that, I'm in charge. She stopped the words on her lips, though. That was Rockie talk and they were past that now. He saved my life. I owe him this, so she nodded. 'Together,' she said.

There was utter silence round them but Dex could imagine his booted feet scrunching in the snow. The space suit felt oddly heavy after moving in a Copy.

It was much slower than he imagined, and even the slight gravity of Triton seemed to weigh heavily.

'Dex,' came Asa's voice, buzzing in his ears, tiny and distant. He tried to speak, but he was faintly aware of that cold water scanning-flow again. His head was buzzing, too. I'm tired, he thought – no sleep, the stress, grandfather and that old rifle.

'Dex, are you all right?'

Asa thumped him on the shoulder and his helmet bonked aginst the solid side of the linker. He nodded. The dizziness seemed to lift. 'I'm OK, Asa.'

If he hadn't looked back at her then he wouldn't have seen it, somehow coming into view before the first faint wisps of pink snow drifted against his helmet. Something that for a disordered moment was four-legged, twice as tall as them with an eye-slitted inhuman face. Dex pointed and Asa turned.

'What's that one?' Her voice was calm but her feet were already moving her back to the ladder.

'Looks the same as the first one, I think.' Dex couldn't believe how calm he sounded, either.

The thing moved. Dex only knew about armour from what he'd seen on the console. The pattern and helmet were more or less the same, but this one sat on something also plated in shaped metal. Something that stamped the frosty ground with sharp hooves and snorted clouds of steam through its nostrils. An Earth horse, covered with armour like its rider. The helmeted head was looking in their direction and the long lance it held swung wickedly down, spear-point gleaming and pennant flapping in the gathering pink storm.

Then it charged.

11   The seige of Castle Miranda

The light gravity of Triton didn't seem to bother the thing at all. Dex and Asa barely turned in a plodding bounce back to the linker and it had already covered half the distance. Frost crackled under the hooves and the armoured knight and his armoured horse gathered speed like a single terrible mechanism of steel. The helmet head showed over a small shield and the spear-point glinted viciously in the driving snow.

Asa was near the ladder now but it was already too close. Even if she got up, Dex would not – that lance would split him like protein on a spike. She stopped and Dex cannoned into her.

'The cords!'

She was already on her knees, grabbing for the parachute cords. Dex realised what she was doing and knelt beside her. The armoured creature pounded up in an exploding cloud of sharp frost. They both grabbed a long cord each and yanked hard. The cords rose, tangling round the horse's hooves. Its mouth opened in a frantic silent whinny and it crashed down sideways before scrambling back to its feet, apparently unhurt. Not so the rider, who sailed out of the high saddle as though from an ejector-seat. He crashed down head first in a jumble of body and limbs, like a collapsed Copy. The little shield cartwheeled awkwardly for a moment, and then fell flat. The lance remained sticking up at a slanted angle in the snow.

'Watch out for others,' said Asa.

She was running stiffly towards where the armoured creature lay. Dex followed, looking round him as he did. The pink snow was thicker now and splattering against them. She knelt and tried to pull the helmet visor up. It wouldn't move.

'Asa, we'd better get back.'

'I want to see its face!'

Another swirl of snow almost hid the linker from view and Dex felt that vague tingle of evil through his body again. Nightmares came out of this pink snow. That thing at their feet was solid and real – but part of a nightmare.

'Asa – let's get back!'

She stopped trying to open the visor and looked up. He could see her eyes wide behind the iron-glass of her helmet and she nodded. As she did, something struck the ground at their feet. Dex looked down. A small, heavy arrow was sticking in the blue frost by his boot. Then another skimmed by.

'Come on!' he yelled.

They ran clumsily back to the steps. Another arrow hit the side of the linker, and suddenly the pink snow was full of deadly whizzing hornets. Dex risked a glance back as Asa pulled him up behind her.

Out of the snow now, a line of things were advancing. They had big square shields and faces covered with close-fitting helmets. As he watched, another stopped and aimed something like a rifle. Another arrow struck the stair rail with vicious force and rocketed through the airlock door as it slid open. Asa pulled him through and the door shut as a volley rapped on Miranda's hull like iron hailstones, warning of the storm to come.

The arrow that came through the airlock with them was about thirty centimetres long, with short flight feathers on one end and a squat heavy point of metal on the other. On Earth it would have been made of wood and metal. This one was a perfect duplicate, but even the short feathers were not real. It was an exact replica, so accurate that Asa was able to date it at once in the computer memory banks.

'Crossbow soldiers, fourteenth century and from the markings on their shields . . .' Asa paused, inputting a moment '. . . Burgundian, a province of Earth France, part of today's Europa land-mass.' She grimaced. 'Most of it classified now as P-rad.'

That meant pollutant-radiation, so there was nothing living now where those soldiers came from and Dex let the arrow drop. 'Every creature we've seen has had its face covered,' he said.

'Maybe they haven't got faces,' said Asa quietly.

'At least I know I'm not crazy.'

'Or we both are.' And I'm really crazy because I keep wanting to tell Dex everything that Cleo said not to, thought Asa. Another bolt whanged off the observation windows. She sat forward in the control chair. 'Those things must know by now that they can't hurt us.'

The crossbow soldiers had lined up in front of the bow section, standing behind their big square shields and firing in turns. Each would then ground the crossbow, set a foot on the bow to keep it in place and wind the draw-string back with a small handle. Another short heavy arrow or bolt taken from a pouch on the belt was then slipped onto the bow. Then up the crossbow would come, the string would twang and the short iron-tipped bolt would viciously spring at the shuttle. The movements of each soldier were as precise and programmed as any android and the bolts bounced off the observation ports and metal sides.

'Sure.' Dex was thinking now too. 'But they've got our attention, haven't they?'

The same thought had occurred to Asa. 'Check the rear.' Dex went and a moment later his shout sent her running.

In the distance, pink snow swirled and splattered as though flicked with an invisible brush. Through it were more of the humanoid things and over them, still half-seen, towered something with grasshopper legs and a huge oval head that nodded horribly in their direction.

'And what the hell . . . is that?' breathed Dex. Asa was already on her way back to the flight deck.

And in a strange way, both knew what they would find before Asa isolated the image in the memory banks. She shook her head in disbelief and said quietly in the same way, 'Oh, by the great red spot of Jupiter, this isn't happening.'

'Trebuchet?' said Dex.

'Trebuchet.' Asa pronounced it 'Traybooshey', shaking her head again as she read the bright lines of data. 'It was a kind of giant stone-thrower, working on a counterweight.' She looked at him. 'Dex, we're besieged. They must think this is a castle.'

'The siege of Castle Miranda?'

'Yes!' She stood up and her eyes blazed like brown fire. 'Dex, this is incredible. Something is simulating those things and using them to contact us!'

'Yeah, with rocks and arrows?'

'Bolts,' said Asa. 'Crossbows have bolts.' She thought a moment. 'I think those soldiers were just driving us back to Miranda.'

'Why— ' He broke off and they both looked out of the port again. The tap-tap tappa-tap of the bolts had stopped and all they could see was pink snow drifting over blue ice. The crossbow soldiers and their square lines of shields had gone. 'Asa, where did they go?'

Something crashed darkly overhead and smashed into the ice with a flurry of blue and pink rising up in a cloud. Asa focused the monitor on-screen. It looked into the cargo hold and then it showed the trebuchet more clearly. The grasshopper legs were big uprights and between them the oval head was being pulled down again.

'They moved out of range,' she said.

Moments later another rock sailed over and crashed down on the ice in line with the first. On-screen, the heavy arm was already being pulled back. That oval thing was spoon-shaped; the rock was loaded into it, the ropes cast off and the heavy counterweight on the other side swung down. Another rock soared over and crashed beside the first two.

'How come they're not correcting their aim?' muttered Dex. 'Ten metres down and they'd be scoring.'

'Hey, shout it through the airlock Dex, they might correct their aim.' Asa scowled as another rock crashed down. 'Come on, whatever they're up to, let's show them who's boss.' She brought a layout graphic on-screen and grinned. 'Good, still there. The crash didn't knock her off.'

97

'Her?'

'Susie.' She smiled again. 'She'll sort them out.' She was programming now and her mouth formed a grin. 'SUSA, Space Utility Surveillance Auxiliary.'

She inputted a release code and something clanked beside the shuttle hull as another rock crashed over. Now the monitor came into life again, the picture moving across the snow. 'We use Susie for probe work, hull maintenance.' She flicked up a graphic of something that looked like a small two-legged bullet, then back to the picture, now moving across snow. 'Susie's got a camera eye, so we can monitor.'

The picture was much closer now to the stalk-legged stone-thrower and ahead, some of the cross-bow soldiers were looking over the top of their shields. Dex flinched as another bolt whanged viciously at the screen, but Asa just smiled. 'Susie's eye can stop a meteor.'

The probe was closer now and suddenly two of the crossbow shields fell over as it barged through them. A sword-blade flashed in front and the armoured legs of a knight were knocked aside. The picture jarred as though blows were being showered upon it and a crossbow soldier tripped and fell in front. His helmet face glared at them, but there was no flash of eyes behind the slits. An axe-blade bounced off the picture, then ahead were the thick uprights of the stone-thrower. Asa smiled again.

'Susie comes with mooring lines,' she said. 'Watch this.' Her hands flicked over the console as she inputted again.

The screen picture changed and another pair of armoured legs were knocked aside. The picture began circling round the wooden uprights and Dex looked back at the cabin monitor, still patched through to where the cargo hold was. SUSA was moving in a plodding scuttle now, round and round the stone-thrower, moving backwards and releasing alloy wire from a metal belly-button. Most of the shields were knocked down, the knights and crossbow soldiers standing in little puzzled groups. Some were still trying vainly to hit it, others were sitting down.

'Now back to Mamma, Susie.'

SUSA began trotting back to the linker, as fast as its little legs would go. Behind it, the alloy wire tightened and SUSA suddenly stopped.

'Come on, Susie.' Asa tapped in full power. Susie stood there for a moment, crossbow bolts skidding off it, then jerked and waddled bravely forward. Behind it, the stone-thrower began to waver and lurch and quite suddenly crashed over into the blue ice.

'Score one for Castle Miranda!' Dex shouted and Asa clapped. Then her grin changed to dismay.

'Oh, poor little Susie. I think she blew her circuits.'

The ice clouds had cleared and the trebuchet was tumbled and broken. Ahead of it, the probe lay on its back, little legs sticking up helplessly in the air. Then the last scraps of pink snow seemed to swirl and settle and pink-gold light flashed on the siege-machine, the soldiers, knight and their scattered equipment. It gleamed like sunset for a moment and everything vanished in the dazzle. Only the churned blue frost and the little probe remained.

'At least we know how it's done,' said Dex quietly.

They went back to the flight deck. Dex fetched

some water and protein biscuits. When he came back, Asa was standing by the observation port, frowning. She pointed to the row of craters made by the trebuchet rocks in the blue snow.

'Why did they space those shots so neatly . . . like a straight line?' She gave a puzzled shrug.

'They didn't exactly have laser sights on that thing, you know.' Dex tried to smile. 'Asa, you were great.'

'You're not so bad either.' They sat down on the flight deck to eat their biscuits, then Asa nearly choked, her mouth full of biscuit. 'Dex . . . is this happening?'

Asa's expression was almost funny, but Dex knew exactly how she felt. The last hour had been too fantastic, too crowded with bizarre happenings, for them to think. But now the fantastic unreality came rushing back.

They had crashed in the broken half of a long-linker on an orbiting moon, millions of kilometres from the nearest space-station. Outside, in temperatures of minus 400°, were soldiers in armour from six hundred years ago in Earth history – apparently alive, apparently breathing the poison methane atmosphere and doing their utmost to break into their Castle Miranda. Soldiers from Earth, a planet that was just an overhead star in Triton's black sky. All parts of a puzzle that made up into nowhere.

Dex finished his coffee and sighed. Opposite him, Asa had fallen asleep with a half-eaten biscuit in her hand. Yes, this was crazy and unbelievable, but he wouldn't share it with anyone else. Friedelinde, Jahudi, even Romhilda – all of them seemed no more real than holograms against this red-brown girl from Pallas who always came back fighting. Dex could remember from history about the Earth pioneers who had explored the forests and oceans. Pioneers like Asa were pushing back the black oceans and black forests of outer space. One last impossible thing was happening to Dex; he was admitting to himself that Asa could have handled this alone.

'I'm a passenger,' he muttered to himself, then closed his eyes and slept.

Suddenly, Dex awoke and looked at the consoles. The time readout showed two hours had passed. Something, a noise, had woken him and he looked up at the screen, still patched through to the cargo monitor – and shouted.

'Asa!'

She sat up blinking and he pointed at the monitor. Asa scrambled at once to her feet and went running clumsily down to the cargo airlock. She looked outside and turned to Dex.

'Seal helmets.'

Dex automatically snapped his shut at the tone of command. Suddenly he realised he didn't mind Asa being in charge – even though on Mars Orbit it would have been unthinkable. They went through to the second airlock and Asa made to look cautiously through the porthole. There was a flash and a burst of smoke as she did and both ducked as something whistled overhead.

'What was that?' yelled Dex.

The drifting pink snow was back, outlining dark figures clustered round something. Then it cleared and they both saw what the something was. Asa's face was pale behind her helmet visor as she turned to Dex.

'*That* is the end of Castle Miranda,' she said.

Out in the snow was a line of soldiers, their flat-brimmed helmets and long trenchcoats from the computer memory banks of World War One. So was the long-barrelled, big-wheeled gun they were gathered round as it flashed and a shell whistled overhead.

'Heavy artillery,' said Dex.

Asa nodded, her face white. 'We shouldn't be able to hear that,' she said. 'Not in almost nil atmosphere pressure.'

Dex nodded, his face white. And, Asa thought, something alien had to be controlling all this. First it has bought up a crude medieval stone-thrower, then a twentieth-century cannon. There was another flash and this time they heard the roar of the explosion as well as the sharp overhead whistle.

'Something wants us to hear,' he said. 'Maybe wants us to give up?'

'That easily, Dex?'

'No.' He tried a brave grin. 'Let's make them say please.' Another shell whistled overhead and exploded beyond the bow section. 'They're still bad shots.'

Asa wasn't certain whether she suddenly guessed, or whether she just felt that first faint tremor underfoot. She turned and ran back to the flight deck, noticing their booted feet were running more easily. Somehow a gravity field was establishing itself; an unknown force was settling round them and that made her run faster. She stopped in the flight deck, looking out of the observation window.

'They're not aiming at us,' she said.

Ahead were the neat craters made by the trebuchet stones. On either side, just as neatly spaced, the crater marks of the exploding shells, but now the straight line was curving at the edges. Another shell landed, bursting into pink, blue and black smoke and now the curve was more obvious. Then a sudden sharp black crack appeared between two of the crater marks; this time, both of them felt that little tremor underfoot.

On the rear monitor was an unmoving group of dark figures, half hidden in the sweeping brush-strokes of pink snow. There were more sharp whistles and explosions and with every flash and bang of the cannon, the line curved more into a U-shape and more black marks split between the craters.

'That thing isn't stupid,' said Dex. 'It's very clever.'

Now Miranda's flight deck was slanting upward. Dex and Asa grabbed each other as they slid down against the back. Asa's coffee spilled and instead of floating up in droplets, it ran over the floor. Gravity was being restored and they stood up, looking out of the observation window. Round them, the blue frost cracked like icing on a cake. Darkness edged between the cracks and the ice slab under Miranda's bow section slanted, the weight of the hull sliding it forward.

Triton was opening a black mouth to swallow them.

12   Down Triton's black throat

The deck angled again, seeming to steady itself, and Asa crawled over the metal floor to the consoles. She punched a code into the console and waited for the readouts to flicker.

'Triton's supposed to be solid,' said Dex as he crawled up beside her.

'Nothing on Triton is impossible,' said Asa. She slammed her hand against the console. 'Three hours at least before Cleo comes over again!'

Miranda tilted again as ahead, the blackness began bubbling over the cracks. 'Some kind of mud,' said Asa. She tapped in another code and there was a clanking sound behind them. 'I freed the parachute unit. Maybe Cleo will see it when she comes over.'

'She won't see us.' They were strapping themselves into the console chairs now. Dex felt oddly calm as they slanted forward again. 'We'll be under by then.'

They braced themselves as Miranda slipped more steeply, but the linker only butted softly as though its deadweight was being thickly cushioned into the blackness. Then it rocked back level again.

'Cleo won't give up,' said Asa quietly.

'Neither will we, Asa.'

Their hands came out and closed together. Miranda jarred and drooped, moving down quickly like an elevator at Mars Orbit. It was silent now; the firing had ceased and they could feel an unseen black level of coldness creeping up the sides of the linker. Neither spoke as the first black edge of mud appeared at the observation port. Miranda kept sinking, slowly and steadily now and Dex shut his eyes. When he opened them again, the blackness was complete.

Asa let go his hand and turned up the lighting. A yellow shade-edged brightness contrasted with the thick suffocating blackness outside and she looked at the console readouts. There was no sensation of sinking now, but she shrugged.

'Still going down,' she said.

'How deep, do you think?' Even as he spoke, Dex knew it was a stupid question. This moon was supposed to be solid – they shouldn't be sinking at all.

'Triton, Dex. Nothing is impossible.'

And it was no use trying to work out how deep we'll go, thought Dex. The stuff was probably a mix of silicate dust and nitrogen, but it was like quicksand, sucking the shuttle farther and farther down. Even though they had an energy reserve for the systems and food and water, that didn't matter. Because neither knew how long Miranda's bows would withstand the pressure of the mud.

'All this is part of a pattern,' said Asa. Her red-brown face contrasted with the yellow shadows.

'The easiest way to kill us?' said Dex. He tried to stop himself breathing heavily because it sounded too scared.

Asa shook her head. 'No, keeping us penned in until they cracked the ice.' She was breathing heavily too. 'That gun could have blown us up any time, Dex.'

'It was just trying to break the ice.' Dex gulped to stop his loud breathing. 'And get us through.'

'Something very clever,' said Asa. 'And it hasn't finished with us yet.'

'At least it seems to want us alive,' muttered Dex.

'Always look on the bright side, eh Rainie?'

She grinned and Dex grinned back. It was the first time she'd used the word in a friendly way and he thought of something. It was an odd, disjointed thing to slip into his mind while the linker sank even deeper into the soft oozing blackness round them.

'Ah . . . those post-sparks from Spoke to Earth . . . you could monitor them all?'

'Yes.' Asa's voice went a little careful. 'By accident of course.'

'I suppose you could monitor us on the open intercom . . . talking about – everything?'

'About Rockies, you mean?'

'Yes. And Sandies, Ice-heads and . . .' Once Dex had used those words so naturally and now they felt awkward and crude on his tongue. 'Anyway, it all sounds pretty stupid now.'

'I know.' She nudged his shoulder. 'So does Rainie.'

'Why do you call Earth people Rainies – Rain-bows?' Once Dex had thought it was because Earth was beautiful and full of colours but there was something in the way that Asa and those miners used it – something different.

Asa watched the readouts for a moment, then breathed heavily. 'Rainbows symbolise Earth for us. A spectrum of beautiful colours, some visible, some not. And a rainbow means real atmosphere, real rain and air to breathe. Then it vanishes.' She was silent for a long time and the readouts flickered. Miranda was more than a hundred metres down now and still sinking. Dex felt a panicky, trapped feeling bubbling inside but Asa went on talking and her voice calmed him. 'Earth is like that to us. Like the bands of a rainbow, levels we can see and levels we can't. Nobody from the solar colonies will ever live there, Earth is the wrong colour for us. So it's like the Rainbow. Something that isn't really there.'

Her words were sad but certain in the yellow darkness. Asa had lifted a tiny corner of her private world and Dex knew that if he spoke, she would seal it shut again. So he waited, listening over the sound of his own breathing and watching the console. Then he pointed. Asa followed the line of his finger and suddenly sat forward, the moment gone. On the console, the pressure and depth readouts were steady at two hundred metres.

They had stopped sinking.

Everywhere on Miranda the deck was steady under-foot as though the bow section was resting on solid rock. And every observation porthole neatly outlined total blackness. Their feet echoed as they walked through the silent yellow-edged darkness and tested the airlock doors. They held, but Miranda did not move. There was nothing to do but go back to the flight deck and wait.

'Hey,' said Asa. 'These are going mad.'

She had patched the power coil readouts into the main console. The readouts were flickering madly like an uneven wavebeat and building themselves upwards.

'How can we be taking on more power?' breathed Dex.

'Energy transmission or something. We must be taking it in from below.'

'Where from? It's — ' Dex had nearly said 'impossible' again and bit the word off in his mouth. 'Asa, what the hell are we sitting on?'

'Let's get a sonic going.' A linker could chart its way through heavy atmosphere by sending out soundwaves that would project back a picture of anything solid ahead. 'I'll program for a square kilometre.'

'Maybe it's natural energy from inside Triton.'

'Maybe.'

It was silly even to suggest it, Dex knew that. Natural energy could not affect the ship like that. They watched as the console screen cleared itself. Dancing pinpoints of green light were dotted all over the screen as the sonic waves began stabbing out like hundreds of probing fingers in the dark. Then Asa screamed loudly.

'Dex!'

He jerked his head up. 'What?'

'Something – I saw a face at the observation port!'

'One of those things from the surface?'

'I don't know, but I saw it. Pressed up very close for a moment.'

'OK, I believe you.' Dex did – Asa was just too strong to let nerves get to her. And there was the sense all round and getting stronger that something was watching them. It was invisible but constant, like a soundless heart-beat in the strange dead silence.

The dancing green dots on-screen were forming

themselves now and Asa inputted a program order to create a graphic. The little click of the buttons under her fingers were like horrible tiny footsteps. Then there was an echo under the footsteps and Dex put out his hand to stop.

'What?' Asa breathed.

'Thought I heard something.' Dex knew that he had, a small scraping echo over the click of the keys. 'No, gone now.'

Asa just nodded as though she hadn't heard. Her body was going stiff and tense and he felt his own stiffen the same way as he looked at the console screen. Because he couldn't believe what he was seeing.

'I'll extend the picture another square kilometre,' said Asa. She did and the click-click of the keys sounded plainly.

'Go to five square k's . . .' said Dex.

Click-click-click went the keys as Asa did so. The screen graphic extended and the green dot pattern went with it, reforming again. 'Five *more* square k's,' said Asa, her voice sharpening in utter disbelief. 'Dex, this isn't happening!'

The sonic wavelengths were spreading out round the ship. As they picked up and returned an image, she matched it to the graphic of their linker. And as the sonic waves spread further and further, she reduced the linker, one kilometre to five, then five more. Then ten after that so the spaceship shrank to insect size on their screen and an 'edge' formed round the screen. By then, sonic wave were reaching some twenty-five square kilometres.

I can see this, thought Dex, but it's not real – nothing like this could exist. But that watching feeling was still running through him, colder than the blackness outside the spaceship, tingling like a nightmare all over his body. Because the 'solid area' that they rested on was octagonal in shape and inset at intervals with sharp circle-topped projections and maze-like markings running in all directions.

'I've seen things like this before, Dex,' Asa whispered.

'Yes, we've got them on Miranda. Much smaller versions.'

He undid the access panel below the console and flipped it out. Inset were dozens of the same thing, but microscopic in size and clustered in their thousands. They were program circuits that carried the electronic thoughts of the spaceship. Link Miranda was resting on a gigantic computer, something so big that it reduced them to pinhead size on an electronic chessboard.

'If that's one circuit,' said Dex, 'I wonder how big the terminal is.' And the answer inputted itself into his mind even before Asa spoke.

'Moon size,' she said. 'Triton.'

A thunderous sound came crashing through the ship like heavy banging. Neither reacted or even felt panic. It was as though they were expecting it, having seen something so incredible that nothing else could scare them.

'Something wants to get in,' said Asa.

Set at floor level in the second flight deck was a wide, round airlock hatch. It led through to another below, for emergency access to the hull. It was shaking as they watched and something clanged below.

'The second hatch just went,' said Asa.

Something was scrabbling around below the hatch.

110

Then the bolts began unlatching themselves, one by one. Each made a deep noise in the smooth dead silence. The last bolt opened and more silence followed.

Then the hatch began to rise.

13 Other-worlds of yesterday

The hatch was a heavy thick lid of steel, coated with
vulcanite and weighing several hundred kilograms.
Now it was lightly opening upward as though an
invisible hand was pushing it back. A black circle
appeared underneath.

'Come on then!' shouted Dex and his hand-clasp
with Asa nearly tore apart.

'They'll come when they're ready.' Asa tightened
her hand again and tried to keep herself resolute.

The hatch was poised full open now, but nothing
happened. The silence stayed dark and an edge of
blackness seemed to spill over on to the deck.

'I think we have to make the next move,' said
Asa. Dex just looked at her and she pointed to
a black overspilling edge of darkness. 'Whatever's
under there wants us to go down.'

'And what if we don't?' As Dex spoke, the darkness crept further over.

'Then that stuff will come up.' Asa looked at the
darkness as though she was tuning to a wavelength
Dex couldn't hear. 'Dex, we haven't got a choice.'

The darkness was like thick black coffee, spilling
up over the hatch. Asa's hand was tight round Dex's
and they took a step forward. The coffee-black stuff
ebbed back a little as they did. They took another
step and it swirled back down the hatch plug-hole,
the metal sides of the airlock gleaming again. One

step back – both of them somehow sensed it – and the stuff would come bubbling up again. Something was holding them close inside the metal shell of their linker, ready to close a black suffocating hand.

Asa began taking off her space suit. She caught Dex's gaping look and snapped, harder than she meant. 'Haven't you noticed?'

Dex stood stock still for a moment and then he did notice. Through Link Miranda now, the strange new sense of heaviness was complete and their space suits were thick encumbering garments on their bodies.

'Gravity,' said Asa.

Whatever force lay under that black coffee stuff was able to make artificial gravity. Not the whirlabout kind of Spoke or Marsbase, but a real gravity they could move in. Dex began taking off his gear and when his fingers hesitated, he forced them to keep going. Asa wasn't showing fear, so he could not. His helmet dropped like the clang of a slamming door.

Asa dropped her own helmet and went to the very edge of the hatch. 'Come on,' she said and put one foot on the ladder. The hatch gaped below her like a black throat.

'Asa . . .' whispered Dex.

Asa knew her face was pale in the yellow-dark shadows. I have to go, Dex, she wanted to say, but the words stayed in her mouth. I am a child of outer space, she said to herself. This thing is part of my awareness even if it destroys me. Her leg seemed made of metal, but she swung a foot out and hooked it on to a lower rung.

Dex came up to the edge and made a half-grabbing motion as though to pull her back. Asa put on her best Cleo-expression and took another step down.

She scowled so fiercely that she actually forgot for a moment that she was challenging the unknown. When she looked back down, the black coffee stuff had ebbed again. 'It wants us to come down,' she said.

Her voice echoed and Asa was annoyed it seemed to quaver. She was even more annoyed when Dex at once jumped over to the top of the ladder, his body outlined in the grey-black track suit.

'Ok, I'm coming,' he shouted.

Well, Super-Dex to the rescue, she thought, and looked down as her boot touched something soft. The coffee stuff had ebbed like clean jelly, sinking below the metal sides of the hatch and forming its own glistening walls of darkness.

'This thing not only makes gravity but its own forcefields,' she said. Her foot was on the last rung of the metal ladder. A mud rung grew below it and Asa tested her foot cautiously. It was solid. She went down further and the bottom sank, while more solid mud rungs grew beneath her feet. Now she was putting her hands on them as well and above, Dex put his foot on the first.

She was at the bottom now, standing on a flat glossy coffee-coloured floor. Asa stamped her foot uncertainly, then more firmly.

'It seems solid enough,' she said.

'And what now?' said Dex.

The black force intelligence seemed to hear him. The dark walls rippled and spread back like a tide going out. Behind they left shapes; overhead was a low, dark ceiling. The shapes formed themselves into sharp edges and flat surfaces, familiar lines that both had seen before.

114

'Dex . . .'

In a sense this was even worse than the unknown. The last edges of darkness slicked away, leaving everything exact, mud-coloured but identical. It was as though the intelligence force was an evil wizard mocking them and playing tricks with their minds. Asa walked forward and looked round. Dex followed. A clear pale light shone through everything, but without casting shadows. There was the low table and the couch where Lan had sprawled asleep. The chair where Cleo had sat, and the other chair Dex had knocked over when Asa punched him. Even the graffiti marks, black against the coffee-mud walls, were there.

It was the linker waiting area at Marsbase where they first met.

'Why is it showing us this?' whispered Asa.

'Something we can relate to?' Dex nearly smiled as he remembered that punch on his jaw. 'Something we can feel comfortable in?'

Asa didn't smile back. She looked round, her face set and frowning. 'What do you want?' she shouted suddenly.

Nothing answered. But out of the silence, a faint trilling sound grew round them. Dex looked up, but the overhead hatch and mud steps had disappeared into the dark coffee ceiling. He looked round slowly, trying to think what an alien intelligence would say to them. How it would speak, how it could even communicate.

'It's logical,' he said. 'That's why it created all this.' Asa looked at him, not sure what he was saying. 'So we have to be logical.'

'How?'

115

'We have to leave this room and go somewhere. That's why it took away the mud steps.'

'How the hell do we go anywhere, then — ' Asa's angry, slightly scared words stopped as she realised what he was saying and she turned.

'Through the door?' she said.

There were two doors in the coffee-mud replica of the waiting area. One was the door from the Marsbase corridor and the other would have led to the shuttle. Dex tried the corridor door first but it was fast and somehow sealed into the mud. Asa turned and walked over to the other door. Her footsteps imprinted silently on to the dark floor and that faint trilling tingled through her body. She waited for Dex to join her, then pressed the handle softly. It moved. She took her hand away for a moment.

'If that thing wanted to hurt us, we'd be dead now,' said Dex.

Asa nodded. 'Here goes.'

She pressed the handle again and the door moved. Asa stepped back and nudged it with her booted foot. Although made of steel, it moved as lightly as the hatch had opened. Asa stood poised on one leg as though frozen, looking incredulously at her boot.

It was splashed with sunlight.

The same sunlight was a square puddle on the dark floor round them. The straight edges of the sun puddle spread as Asa put her foot down and pushed the door open further. Then, as though tuning to a new wavelength, they heard sounds, strange chattering sounds that Asa did not recognise.

'Birds.' Dex spoke behind her. 'That's the sound of birds.'

He put his hand out beside hers. Together they

116

pushed the door wide open, flinching as warm sunlight hit them with the shock of a blow. Together they walked through.

Asa flinched again, turning her face away as the sunlight dazzled like a laser wave. It came from a beautiful golden sun in an incredibly blue sky. Even for Dex, this sun was different to the savage scorching one he knew from Earth, when it shone through the clouds; the sun he could only look at through a filter. This was strong and hot, full of gentle power. Beside him, Asa looked from the blue and dazzling gold down to another beautiful strong colour – the green grass under her feet.

Walls of grey stonework covered in green and brown creeper extended in a wide enclosure and over to one side was a high arched gate of wrought iron. Dex looked at Asa, but she was already walking forward as though in a trance.

Ahead of her were a row of bushes. Asa had seen small bushes in the greenhouse on Pallas but this one was as tall as her, luxuriant, thickly green and clipped fantastically into the shape of a bird. Other bushes were clipped as animals, ovals or balls. The noise level sharpened loudly, seeming to burst like a full orchestra round them as they walked through the bushes. Ahead was a scene so unreal that they stopped, their mouths open with astonishment, letting the warm sun beat on their faces because what lay before them could not exist.

But it did.

Ahead was a group of women. They were dressed in fantastic costumes, so splendid and magnificent that they were almost alien – long-sleeved, full-skirted dresses of shining colours, embroidered with gold and silver thread that flashed and sparkled in the sunlight. Their faces were covered with a thick paste of make-up and their hair was up in towering ornate creations set with flowers and jewels. Unconsciously Asa put up a hand to her own thick untidy hair and tried to imagine rouge plastered on her cheeks, but it was impossible. Too unreal.

The women in their billowing dresses were gathered round four children. The girls were miniature copies of the women and the boys in bright short jackets and pantaloons of an Earth material Asa had never seen. Dex had, though – it was silk, something nobody wore any more. Beside them stood a man in a long black coat, his hair cut and shaped like a wig and powdered white. He was playing an instrument Asa recognised but had never seen, a violin. It was varnished golden brown and etched with gilded paint that flashed in the sunlight. His fiddle arm moved up and down and he capered on thin, white-stockinged legs to the piping notes of music.

'Something . . .' Asa paused because her words sounded too strange to pass her lips '. . . out of Earth history?'

'Seventeenth/eighteenth century Europe, I think,' whispered Dex as though afraid they would hear him. Nobody had seen them yet. Over to one side, by the high wrought iron gates, was a row of other women in long dark gowns and with white caps enclosing their hair. They stood quietly, hands clasped and heads bowed as though afraid of intruding. Servants of some sort, thought Dex, but there was something wrong. The ladies, the children and the fiddler were a little to one side but behind them, the row of

118

maidservants faced Dex and Asa directly. But they showed no signs of surprise at seeing two strangely clad teenagers standing in front of them.

Asa and Dex began walking slowly forward over the lovely green grass. Warm golden sun beat down out of the blue sky and ahead the children danced. The ladies were laughing and talking softly among themselves in a strange language, but there was almost a shrill, tense note to their enjoyment. Each held an exquisite painted fan in a white-gloved hand, moving it constantly – restlessly? Asa was sensing a strained undercurrent to this. Then the four children formed a line and turned, dancing forward, their happy eyes directly watching Asa and Dex as they danced forward. The women turned, too, fans fluttering, and the fiddler's wide brown eyes looked at them but he played on, a gold-buckled black shoe tapping on the green grass.

'They can't see us,' whispered Asa, but so loudly that the group must have heard. 'Dex, they can't see us.'

The fiddle sent high pealing notes into the sky and the children reformed into a circle. To one side was a marble fountain set with bronze fish spouting thin crystal streams from their mouths. And beside this was a huge gilded wooden cage, filled with tiny yellow birds that twittered in a background melody to the notes of the fiddle. But again Asa sensed it, that tense desire for enjoyment as though building it like a screen to protect themselves – to keep something out?

Asa knelt suddenly and tried to break off a blade of grass. Then she tried to pull the head off one of the yellow daisies. 'Not real grass or flowers,' she

119

said. She stood up again. 'So why are we being shown this?'

'Listen,' said Dex.

Somewhere, another sound level was building. There was the fiddle music, the laughter of the children and low conversation of the adults. The splashing tinkles of fountain water and the bird melody. Through it that faint trilling sound, so low they could scarcely hear it, but now the other sound level was rising, a sound like confused shouting. Asa nodded; she could hear it now.

Then the caged birds stopped singing. The fiddler stopped, too, his fiddle bow still poised. The children stopped dancing and the women stopped fluttering their fans. Then the shouting became suddenly louder and the line of manservants broke uncertainly and scattered as the wrought iron gates burst open and a mob of people rushed in. They were in rags. Their hair was tangled, their faces thin and pale, eyes wide and filled with hate. Leading them was a woman in a torn, dirty white dress and long red bonnet. In one hand she waved a long-bladed hatchet.

The ladies were screaming, dropping their fans and blundering into each other in their full skirts as they tried to get away. A maidservant grabbed one of the children, then tripped on the hem of her long skirt. The black-clad fiddler stood bewildered, fiddle bow still raised, when a stone came out of nowhere and struck him on the forehead. He collapsed, fiddle and bow flying in the air. There was confusion and screaming. Asa ducked as another stone flew overhead.

'Dex!'

She had half-turned as she ducked and she grabbed

120

his arm, pointing back. Dex turned. They had come through an entrance in the wall into all this. But through the bushes now there was no sign of any door, as though grey stonework had sealed itself over.

They were trapped.

14 Garden-storm

The mob was spreading out now. Their faces were
pitted, marked with sores and with the skin stretched
tightly over bones. There were children with them,
running forward like yapping dogs among the stumbling rich ladies, pulling at their jewels and orna-
ments. Two children jumped into the fountain and
began splashing each other, screaming happily. A
woman, clutching a baby in a ragged shawl, knelt
and, picking up the fiddle, began to smash it against
the ground. A man, his face red and pock-marked,
pulled off the unconscious fiddler's shoes, wrenching
off each gold buckle with his teeth and spitting them
into his hand.

'Come on,' said Asa quickly.

'Where?'

'There!'

She was pointing over the garden to the wall
opposite. Inset was a small arched door under a stone
archway. 'And let's not get anywhere near them.'

'Why not?' he said.

Asa just pushed him impatiently. 'Explain later –
come on!'

The woman with the hatchet was chopping at the
birdcage. The woodwork splintered under the steel
edge of her hatchet, then she grabbed a piece and
pulled hard. Her face was set in a twisted fury.
The bars came away and the yellow birds began

flying out, fluttering into the air and screeching their melody. She screamed with laughter and waved her hatchet in the air. A man kicked over the table and sat down, cramming the cakes and fruit into his mouth. Another seized the little blue and gold cups and began smashing them, howling with glee. Round him, the strawberries were trodden in a mush underfoot.

Dex and Asa circled round and began running for the opposite door. The ladies and children had disappeared among more of the shaped bushes and the mob swirled round like dry leaves in a storm. Then something crashed into Dex and he was knocked over. Asa pulled him to his feet.

Men appeared, dressed in long blue coats, the same colour as the maidservants' gowns. They carried long wooden staffs tipped with iron and a series of small fights broke out. More of the mob were swirling in like ragged leaves. Asa and Dex ran quickly, zigzagging round the scuffling groups. Asa tripped on the splintered fretwork of the cage and a last trapped bird flew squawking up.

The woman in the red cap was still swinging around with her hatchet. Two servants pushed their staffs at her and she went down, her long skirt flying. One of the men brought his pole back to hit her and Asa stopped to grab it. Her weight and strength should have torn it from his hands, but the swing continued as though nothing had happened. She was flicked away, crashing back into Dex. The trilling sound was louder, he noticed as they went down together.

The red-capped woman swung up from the ground, her hatchet chopping through one iron-tipped pole. The other man raised his pole. Then on the ground, the maidservant who had been knocked over trying to rescue a child, suddenly grabbed his legs. He went over, his pole swing missing. The red-capped woman jumped to her feet, pulling the maidservant up and both screamed over the noise, embracing each other. Dex and Asa kept running, past the broken splashing fountain and Dex's boot crunched on the remains of the fiddle. Without thinking, he bent down and picked up the fiddle bow.

The door was ahead and Asa's hand slammed on the iron handle. It swung lightly open and they dived through the door together, a rock banging on the stonework overhead as they did. Behind them, everything shut as though noise and sunlight had slammed into dark silence. Dex picked himself up from a coffee-dark floor and looked round.

'Back where we started,' he said.

'That was a riot of some sort, eighteenth century, I think,' said Asa. She opened and closed her hands as though feeling the staff being torn from them. Dex was still holding the fiddle bow and he dropped it to the floor. 'Oh, those poor people.'

'Who, the ladies and their kids?'

'No, the others!'

'Asa, they were animals! Did you see that woman waving an axe?'

'And did you see their faces? They were starving. If my kid was hungry then I'd wave an axe too. The rich people had too much and— '

Asa stopped. They were shouting about nothing because it was over. She had a sense that if she re-opened that door, everything beyond it would be gone. And she'd been about to say, Like Earth has too much and the solar colonies want more. She somehow sensed that their unseen watching force wanted her to say that.

'Careful, Dex. That lot could have killed us.'

'How?' Dex got slowly to his feet and collapsed into one of the coffee-coloured chairs. 'How?'

'Did you see me trying to stop that man swinging the stick? Or those rocks just missing us? Or even trying to pull the head off that flower?' She sat down on the couch. 'I think anything that hit us would have gone right on through.'

Dex just nodded. He got up and went over to a coffee-coloured water machine. He pressed a button, then banged it, but nothing worked. 'So what do we do now?' He went back and, without thinking, slapped his hand on her shoulder.

Asa glared. 'Keep your hands to yourself, Rainbow!'

'I'm just saying we have to be careful— ' Rockie, he nearly said. The trilling sound came back round them.

'You're not so bloody careful,' shouted Asa. 'I nearly got myself killed because you forgot your hel-met – all the same rules apply to Spokies, you know!'

Both of them realised they were shouting at the top of their voices. Dex's knees felt suddenly weak and he sat down before he collapsed, not wanting to show weakness in front of Asa. 'We make decisions together,' he said in a low voice.

'What are you whispering for? Afraid the thing will hear us?'

She was still pushing, so Dex pushed back. 'I'm senior to you, Asa.'

'Oh yes? Because you were once up on Spoke, looking down at us like ants in a bottle?'

'No, I— ' Dex stopped and shook his head. 'Hey, what's happening? None of this mattered on the linker.'

'Maybe your Earth psyche is catching up with you.'

Then Asa stopped, too. The trilling sound had become a little louder and she shook her head. She was still angry and Dex knew she was as scared as him. She looked at the door.

'I think we have to open that again.'

Cleo sat tensely at Link Miranda's rear controls. The engineer chair was more narrow and less comfortable than her own. Rek was talking behind her as he scanned.

'No reports. No reports.'

If we had a Copy we could go down and look properly thought Cleo, but the Copy suits are – were – in the front half and—

'They should be sending out a crash signal,' said Lan beside her. His lazy grin had gone completely.

Cleo nodded. Miranda's rear half bucked a little and she looked through the long rear ports at the blue surface of Triton, the blue-green mass of Neptune behind it.

'Full steering restored,' said Lan.

Cleo nodded again and unstrapped herself. They could steer Miranda now and take it back to Mars. It would be a long, long ride in half a linker but they could do it. Rek's voice came in on her thoughts. 'No readings yet.'

'There have to be readings – even crash readings!' Rek bent over his console, but shut his eyes tight a moment. Cleo put out her hand and gently touched him. 'Rek, I know you're doing your best.'

He nodded without looking up. Lan spoke again, quietly. 'There might be nothing left to make a reading.'

'I've got the settings,' Rek yelled. He brought it up on the console, the picture misting and flickering as he did.

'Enhance,' said Cleo. She looked at the on-screen picture and shook her head. 'Are you sure those are the right settings?' But she knew that before Rek double-checked the settings and nodded.

On-screen was the tangled mass of the parachute and beside that, a large semicircle. Something had punched through the ice-crust, forming a black mass of mud, already frosted with blue.

'No wonder there's no signal if it sank in that lot,' said Lan.

'Must have gone deep,' said Rek. He shut his eyes again and rubbed a hand over his red-brown face.

Lan was speaking slowly with practical emphasis. 'We can patch our deep sleep through to the life pods. But it will take more time get back. That means we have to start now.'

Cleo was looking at the tangled parachute mass and the mud semicircle. Asa and Dex were under there. To her surprise she felt something for Dex, even though he was just an arrogant you-be-damned Rainie. He had pulled off an incredible rescue when he saved Asa, but now it was ended for them both. Nothing could have survived an impact like that. She didn't want to speak at first because her voice was trembling. Then she realised it didn't matter if they saw her tears because Rek's hands were still over his face and Lan was looking sideways out of the porthole.

'Is that blasted tel-spark working yet?' she said.

'No. Probably got bashed by the front end of – Miranda.' Lan's voice caught and he did not turn from the porthole.

'All right. Set a course for Mars and begin deep sleep.'

Cleo lay back in her chair and did the strap more tightly. She blinked, letting the tear roll down and felt very tired. Triton was still passing on-screen but she couldn't bring herself to look at it yet. The life pods would keep them alive, but it would be a long, long ride back to Mars. She couldn't wait to lose herself in sleep, even though the loss would still be there when she woke up again.

Dex and Asa were standing side by side. The door was open now and they had forgotten their argument. Behind, also unnoticed, the trilling sound had subsided to an almost unheard pitch. They were even more scared, but neither would show it to the other. It was a quiet, cold fear because what they were looking at now was even stranger than the howling madcap confusion of that sunlit garden of long ago. Something that didn't make sense at all.

The door had swung lightly open. And instead of warm golden sunlight, a pale oblong of moonshine outlined itself on the glossy dark floor. They knew it was moonshine because the moon itself was framed in the black entrance.

We are looking at Earth's moon, thought Dex, and all the features are outlined beautifully because it is such a clear night. He could even see the crater where Moonbase Copernicus was, whose lights at night sent a signal to Earth. There was no signal in the crater now, because they were looking at the moon long before a base was built there.

'How long ago?' he whispered aloud.

Something else hung directly in the entrance, something like a spiked black bony finger, crooked at them as though attached to an unseen skeleton hand and arm. Below was a wood-framed step and above that, a wall of dark, stacked, uneven outlines. The silence was as dark and cold as that black spiky finger beckoning them onward.

All right, thought Dex, we have to know what's behind that thing. He took a step forward into the pale moonshine oblong. Beside him, at the same time, so did Asa. Their hands brushed; they wanted to clasp, but both still remembered that argument. So they walked forward, their bodies jamming in the narrow doorway at the same time. Asa pushed ahead, but tripped on the low wooden step. She stopped for a moment to recover, pushing up the black bony finger as she did.

Dex paused and touched it as he went past. It was wire with sharp points sticking out like long claws, each tipped with a frosting of ice. He ducked underneath and joined Asa on the top stair. The uneven stacked outline was a wall of packed bags and Asa was passing her hands over it as he joined her. They were thick stuffed cloth bags and, like the wire, coated with ice. Small holes were punched into them and the stuffing inside had oozed out. It was made up of grainy particles that Dex had once seen at the construction site of a sea city. The city where he should be with Friedelinde right now, a million miles across space.

'Sand,' he whispered. He rubbed the grainy particles between forefinger and thumb and opened his hand to show Asa. She nodded without looking, intent on something ahead.

In another sandbagged alcove stood a man, so silent and unmoving that Dex thought for a moment it was a statue made out of dark ice. The hands were encased in thick woollen mittens and held a rifle and long bayonet. Dex had seen a rifle like that before. He had dug it out of blue snow, above on Triton's surface, and he had seen the same type held in his grandfather's shaky old hands. A Springfield and bayonet. Instead of sunlight there was an utter freezing cold and the sandbag lines zigzagged away on either side. There was no need to tell Asa they were back in the trenches of World War One. She knew it the same moment he did.

Then in the black sky overhead a red star burst, spilling droplets of bright crimson blood-fire into the darkness.

1. Blood-light and frost-fire

Another red star burst, scattering off more of the glowing crimson. A flare, thought Dex, some kind of signal shot perhaps? He looked back, but the dark ice soldier had not moved even though the red light was beating on his face. Perhaps the flare was just a warning. Asa nudged his hand and pointed sideways.

There, the sandbagged trench wall angled again round a sharp corner. Narrow planks ran along the ground, squelching through the cracks with thick mud and the unmoving soldier had his heavy mud-stained boots planted on one. They had to move on, Dex knew that, but he paused for just a fascinated moment to look up from the mud-stained boots, the legging straps above them and the hem of a battered thick raincoat. His body was criss-crossed with straps and clips of sharp little objects – bullets, Dex knew. Over the high collar, a square unshaven face looked out under the shadow of a flat-brimmed metal helmet. The gas-mask – goggleyes and snout nose of his nightmares – hung by his side, ready for use. Quite suddenly the soldier turned in their direction and spoke.

'Sergeant!'

A large bulk shouldered between Dex and Asa, so roughly that they were thrown to each side of the trench. It was another helmeted soldier, also wrapped in a trenchcoat. The two murmured in low tones and a thick-sleeved arm pointed up at the sky. 'OK, son, keep looking,' they heard the sergeant say. It was flat, drawling and sounded as if drawn out on a slow disc. That's English, thought Dex, spoken the way his ancestors spoke it a hundred and fifty years ago.

The sergeant slapped the soldier with a heavy-mittened hand and went on down the trench. Asa was nudging him again, this time jerking her thumb back. He turned. The doorway they had come through was gone; there were only packed immovable rows of sandbags. Asa pressed one to illustrate her point then pointed ahead again, her lips forming in a wry smile. We have no choice again, said that smile.

'May as well find out where we're supposed to go,' she whispered.

'Find out what something wants us to see,' muttered Dex back. They were billions of kilometres from Earth but standing in the middle of Earth history again. And instead of sunlight, a bitter blue-black cold was freezing through their bodies.

They began to move. The narrow trenchboards stayed rigid under their feet, not squelching with movement as they had when the sergeant trod on them. Then another red signal exploded in the sky, descending slowly with a hissing sound they could distinctly hear. This one changed colour into a ghastly green as it came down; there was a muttering from unseen voices round them and the sergeant's hard, low, 'Shut your mouths!'

Ahead of Dex was another long-coated soldier. A thick scarf was wound round his face, the tin helmet jammed on top. His cheeks were chapped and bleeding, his eyebrows and thick moustache frosted with ice. He was standing on a step built in the side of the trench, his head and shoulders over the sandbag wall, a machine-gun before him. He kept turning the thick, long-snouted barrel like a steel nose sniffing in all directions. His breath made frosty little clouds over his mittened hands. Sitting beside him on the same step was another soldier. A long-barrelled rifle leaned against the sandbag wall beside him and he was using the tip of his bayonet as a spoon to eat from a small tin held in thickly wrapped hands. His boots were bursting open at the toes.

A part of Earth history, thought Dex, preserved intact like a hologram-disc, but alive and solid-real unlike any hologram. A history disc that moves, lives and sounds round us and lets us walk through so long so we don't get in the way.

'Spectators,' whispered Asa behind him.

She was right, thought Dex, we are part of this but only watching it. He stepped round another soldier, huddled on the ground with his head between his knees, helmet in one hand. We are part of this but like a hologram circus and the bright-coloured hologram clowns cannot see us. But these clowns were clad in dark thick clothes, holding heavy, old-fashioned weapons and waiting for trouble.

They were passing the entrance to a small earth-walled room, dug out of the trench. It was framed with heavy slabs of wood and inside flickered the tiny gleam of a candle. A man was seated writing by the light, his movements uncertain and clumsy as though his hand was shaking. He had a pale, sharp face outlined in the candle flame and his eyes were half-closed as if he was nearly asleep. Ahead of them a rat ran squeaking and a rifle butt came down out of the shadows with a heavy thud. It was only a small noise but, ahead, the sergeant whispered savagely again.

They kept walking. Asa stumbled again, flinching at the noise although nothing round them could hear. She kept looking round because this was Earth, the Earth she had never known. It was a strange land from long ago, a different planet and all that she recognised were the stars overhead. She had never set foot on this planet, in this time or any other. This place was cold, unhappy and tense, and the garden before it was sunlit, rich and pathetic; all of it was beauty and life used for the wrong reasons, all of it gone now and wasted. These soldiers were waiting to waste things too, she thought – their lives. She passed another sentry, standing in a trench angle, looking up at the black sky and waiting for something to happen.

Ahead of her, Dex stopped and Asa stumbled into him. He half-turned, his hand finding hers. His fingers were icy cold and she could feel his body shaking against hers, in the thin track suit. Rainie and Rockie, she thought, but right now we need each other more than anything in the universe; they just had to keep going.

The trench stretched on ahead, turning sharply, each angle set with the ribbed frosted sandbags, stretching in bitter cold lines round more corners. Now there were more soldiers, all waiting as though frozen in place. Red-rimmed eyes under flat-brimmed helmets, thickly wrapped hands closed round long-barrelled rifles and sharp steel bayonets, glinting in the frost. More machine-guns and once, in another angle, a low squat metal tube set on a heavy steel plate. Dex had seen that on the computer recall when he was searching for the rifle – a trench mortar that would lob shells up and overhead, down into the darkness beyond the tangled wire. Everywhere, that same tense silent waiting.

'They're expecting something to happen,' said Asa.

The silence went on, but she had the feeling it was going to break at any moment. Overhead were constellations, Ursa Major, Leo and Gemini and she tried to think. They would come out in Earth Europe skies. But the cold of winter was still cutting through this spring like one of those sharp-edged bayonets.

Another red star exploded in the blackness and this one burned into yellow. Another soldier suddenly shouldered ahead of them on to the trench step. There were movements, muttered exclamations and a click-click-clicking sound as soldiers came out of the shadows and pulled back the bolts on their rifles. Another red light zoomed into the blackness and burned into yellow. Ahead somewhere in the frozen darkness came a single rifle shot, followed by a heavy boom like a cannon firing. Overhead came a sharp whistling shriek, then hell unchained itself round them.

The whistling cut and something hit the trench, exploding and scattering the sandbags in solid chunks, crashing down on the trenchboards ahead. Rifle fire burst into a different set of explosions and behind them, the machine-gun opened up with a deafening noise like ripping cloth. Something else stitched a row of neat holes in the sandbags overhead and Dex dived into one of the dugouts, dragging

135

Asa after him. Even as he did, a soldier went running past and his booted foot hit her painfully on the knee.

'How do we get out of this?' she yelled.

Dex paused before answering. The noise was worse now and flares were splotching the black sky like splatters of blood. The torn-cloth sound ripped deafeningly round them and criss-cross lines of white darted in all directions like little seam stitches in the darkness. 'This is really bad,' he yelled above the din. 'If one of those old lead bullets hits us, it'll *really* go through.'

'So what is the force thing trying to do – kill us?' shouted Asa back.

'Maybe it doesn't *know* we can be hurt!' yelled Dex. 'Did you ever think about that?'

A man crashed past their entrance, shouting and ducking as vicious stitch lines of bullets hit the parapet. In the near distance they could hear the sharp sound of bugles and whistles. A soldier blundered up and crouched under the overhang, pulling a bayonet from his leather scabbard. His hands fumbled as he tried to fit it to the rifle. Then he dropped it, covering his face with gloved hands and shaking uncontrollably. Something else exploded overhead and a rat ran squealing from underneath.

'Come on!' yelled Asa. As she spoke, a loud flash lit up the overhead parapet and a man stood there in different uniform and spiked helmet. He leapt down, then another followed him, and another. Asa ducked past him, dragging Dex behind her, thumping into the sides as more of the different-uniformed soldiers jumped down. Behind were screams, yells and the clank of steel on steel. The crimson flares gleamed bloodlight everywhere and ahead the trench ended in another slitted doorway.

'There!' shouted Dex.

Then ahead another soldier jumped down. The overhead bloodlight glinted on his spiked helmet and his eyes glittered underneath. He lunged forward. Asa and Dex jumped each to one side, but this time a boot caught Dex painfully on the shin. The soldier was attacking someone behind and Dex picked himself up, skidding on the frozen trenchboards. Something was rolling ahead of him, landing out of nowhere. He had seen one of those things too, when he was hunting for the rifle on the computer visuals. Asa was kneeling beside it, pulling him up.

'Grenade!' he yelled.

He dived over the grenade and tried to pick it up. It just kept rolling, nearly jamming his fingers. He crouched, shouting, 'Run, Asa, into the dugout.' Her strong hand hooked into his belt and pulled him up. They both jumped for the doorway and jammed together into it. Asa went through first and Dex tumbled after her. Behind the grenade exploded and Dex flinched as the sharp flash came directly at his face. But something crazy was happening. The door lintel and sides were shaking with the force and they could see chunks of sharp metal exploding towards them. But slowly and more slowly still, seeming to stop and skid over an invisible glass wall. Asa gasped with relief.

'We're through the door, out of there,' she said as the whole bloodlit fire-streaked darkness went into the total black of nothing and the screaming, exploding confusion faded suddenly into silence. Dex stood up, nursing his shin and looked round. They were back in the coffee-mud waiting area.

'Hey, do you know how dangerous all this is?' he yelled.

'Yes, and what about you throwing yourself on that grenade?' Asa shouted back.

'So what's the matter with looking after your friends?' he yelled again.

Nothing, I was going to jump on it myself, Asa nearly said. Then she just shook her head and made herself smile. She pulled Dex to his feet and let him lean on her. 'I mean this force thing doesn't want us to get killed,' she said.

'Then what's it doing, Asa?'

'Testing us?' Dex just looked at her, standing on one foot and trying to nurse his shin.

'Dex, did you notice that trilling sound? It was with us all through the trench.'

'No,' said Dex shortly.

'It was. It's a signal . . . a monitoring signal.' Asa didn't know why she said that, it just popped into her mind. At the same time, the trilling sounded again, almost unheard around them. 'I think we were being shown something . . . or something was trying to reach us.'

'How?'

'Both the same . . .' Asa felt her voice go up and down. 'Different ages but the same.' The trilling sound had become a hum, even louder.

'Asa, are you all right? *What* was the same about them?'

Asa couldn't talk now. It was as though there was a hand in her mouth holding on to the words. The walls were quivering out of focus. She could see Dex standing there with a hand to his head. She could feel the power waves building in her body. It was so clear that her own loud voice was ringing in her ears. But fine curtains of gauze seemed to be dropping round Dex and he had his back turned. Dex, this isn't right, turn round—

Dex couldn't hear Asa any more. He felt a pounding rise in his head and the room rippled blackly for a moment as though everything was melting. He blinked and turned round, beginning to speak.

'Asa, what do you mean?'

He stopped. Asa had vanished.

16   The ghost-maker

'Seeing you . . . Asa.' The new voice that spoke to
Asa came from inside and outside. It touched her
tongue and tingled on her face. It spoke uncertainly, as though human sound itself was strange.
Even her name sounded like the distant echo of an
alien shore.

'Seeing me . . .?' she repeated, looking round her.

The coffee-coloured replica of the waiting area
was gone. Asa was standing somewhere else and she
sensed that almost the very dimension had changed.
The floor had become pink and golden and the
walls were only wreathed and misty streamers of
purple-pink light that sometimes wavered upright
and sometimes seemed to walk round her as though
the very room itself was constantly changing. They
gave a feeling of utter depth and through everything,
tiny almost unseen threads of pure light floated
up and down. They were set with flashing sparks
and coiled through the purple-gold mist, sometimes
criss-crossing like a web.

'Seeing you . . . Asa.'

Without meaning to, she put out both her arms
and felt a presence, warm, unseen and very powerful touch her hands and wrap lightly round them
like another hand clasping gentle-tight. A force, a
mind-force, something reaching out but it doesn't
quite know how to contact me.

'How am I . . . speaking?'

'You are speaking in my mind,' whispered Asa. 'You are showing me the different levels of emotion.' The purple-pink walls went deeper, then streaked with dazzling glints of pink-red gold. 'Now I am tuned to them.' There was nothing, but the swirling purple mist came more strongly and one of the tiny golden-dot threads dropped delicately in front and hung over her outstretched hand. It stayed a moment, wonderfully cool and strong and then vanished like ice melting.

'Asa . . . where's Dex?' The voice whispered with a light puzzled note.

'Dex doesn't understand yet.' The voice hummed through her mind and the force touched her face, light and clumsy like a child. 'He doesn't understand yet. You still have to open his mind.'

'Open . . .?'

'Show him more of what you showed me,' Asa whispered, although she knew the force would hear even if she only spoke the words in her mind.

'Ghost things. Show you . . . new.'

The scene round her flash-melted into change. The purple mist pillars became the sharp outlines of a vast landscape, alien to anything Asa had seen – green swirling sky and a crystal ground round her. Crystal spikes towered up into the air, uneven lines and huge rocks, flashing green and yellow then mixing down into a deep green-blue like frozen ocean waves. This time, though, she had more sense of a vision passing round her and could not even feel the blue-yellow diamond pebbles under her feet. Through the green sky shone a greener sun.

'Showing you,' said the voice.

141

The scene was change-melting again and now she was in a tall forest, huge massive trees with blue-green trunks. Overhead was a patch of blue-green sky with two yellow suns in it. Everything seemed filtered with the blue-green except for huge piles of pulpy red fruit that lay on the ground round her.

'Showing me,' she breathed, feeling the sense of wonder build inside her. This time she could breathe the air, it was rich and heavy as though filled with strange spices and the sunlight was sticky and close. The huge trees stretched away in avenues and in the distance, something long and tubular was coiling and passing between them like a giant blue-green worm.

'Show more,' said the voice.

And Asa was standing on a wide, empty plain. In the distance, hundreds of things with rounded shells, like tortoises, were moving. She could breathe this air, too; it was thin and sour-smelling and she almost floated as she walked. Beside her, a long gaping seam of rock had ripped open showing gleams of gold and silver metals below as though the riches of the planet were bursting through. Ahead, the tortoise things opened their rounded shells into giant thick wings and she could hear loud honking sounds as they flapped ponderously into the air.

No other human has ever seen these things, she thought. Asa knew this was only a tiny corner of the immense visuals waiting to unfold, a tiny gleam of sun-fire searing gloriously round her as the scene began to melt-change again. Even now, though, she had time to wonder where Dex had been sent this time.

*   *   *

'You are trying to make me go through that door?' Dex was really angry now and getting no answer made him shout louder. 'Not until you tell me what happened to Asa!'

Silence hung heavy and – he sensed – mocking in the air round him. The waiting area seemed closer, warmer, and the lines seemed to blur for a moment. Dex felt himself getting angry. This force thing might think it was all-powerful, but he was from Planet Earth, he was a two-legged human and this thing needed *reminding* of that!

'I'm from Earth and you are just inside one little cold sore orbiting a useless hunk of rock and gas. Earth owns the solar system and can wipe you any time it wants to!'

The floor was getting sticky underfoot. Dex kicked at the wall and a blob of coffee-mud appeared on his boot. Suddenly the mud floor slopped over his boots and he stepped forward to the new door that had appeared; at once the floor became more solid and Dex became more angry.

'Oh yeah! I go through the door or I sink, right?' The floor became sticky again and Dex took an impatient step forward, feeling it go solid as he did. 'Yes,' he shouted again. 'But I am only going through that door to find out what has happened to Asa. And if I don't find her, we are into *serious* explanations!' Boiling with anger and just to impress the force thing, he walked over, kicked the door open and stormed through.

The first thing that happened was that he hit his head hard and very painfully on a low stone lintel. The blackness became blacker for a moment, then through the sharp dark moment of pain came a horrible smell as though everything dead and rotten had exploded round him. He tried to stand and banged his head on the stonework again.

Dex went to his knees. There were hard rounded stones under his knees and the horrible rotten smell became even worse. All his raging human pride was lost in the dizzy pain blackness and Dex cupped both hands over his head again before he slowly stood up.

There was sunlight now, but thin and pale as though it had filtered a long way to light this darkness. It shone on the rounded stones under his knees, on brick and plasterwork walls, leaning overhead and lined with pressing frowns of black timber. Above that, steep, sharp-angled roofs of red tile, so close that the sky was only a blue bar between them.

The ground was crushed stone and paving. Beside him was a narrow wooden door, set with iron clasps. Beside it was a long window with small dark panes of glass set inside a criss-cross pattern of lead strips. The step from door to ground was packed earth and beside it was a stinking mass of old rags. On the stone paving all round were piles of the stinking brown stuff that animals used to leave behind them – when there were animals on Earth. Waste, manure, whatever it was called, Dex realised that the force thing had dumped him amongst it and also remembered – too late – that it was much more powerful than him.

Ahead was a sharp rectangle of bright sunlight, noise, colour and confusion. He was in an alley, so narrow that both sides pressed against him. It stank and the narrow strip of sunlight overhead burned in slanting dark shafts through the dust and stench. The sharp rectangle opened into a street and framed in it, two children appeared for a moment. Both were dressed in layers of rags, their heads enclosed in wrapped cloth and one swung something as she chased the other, shrieking with laughter. She was holding a dead dog by its tail.

Dex got up and walked to the end of the alley. The stench did not lessen as he felt sunlight on his face. He was in a street more narrow than the corridors of Marsbase. It was paved with square flat lumps of rock and an open ditch ran down the centre. Close buildings of wood, plaster and stone lined each side, the second storey leaning out to cast a strip of black shadow below.

And the people! They were crowding and jostling everywhere. Men in long drab gowns, arguing. Women in long dresses of more colour, their heads wrapped in white cloth. A grey-bearded old man in a black robe wagged his finger at a small group of listeners. Children ducked everywhere, while men and women with bright anxious faces stood behind stalls laid with food and trinkets. And everywhere, a full deafening shout of many voices yelled their presence in a tongue Dex did not understand.

'Oh, great,' he muttered. 'I'm right back in silly bloody Earth history again.'

But this day – somewhere from the past – was special, he could see that. Long gaudy banners hung from each window and at the corner was a wooden statue of a woman with a calm pale face, a hammered circle of brass set above her head. Dex had seen that before, in illustrations of Earth saints. So this was a holy day – holiday as they were later called. Then the drab and brightly clothed people scattered and Dex stiffened against the alley wall as a memory of nightmare rode into view.

He had seen that knight before, and his horse, the ornate, fluted shaped steel plates covering man and animal. That sharp steel helmet face looking from side to side, steel-gloved hands holding the reins tight and forcing the horse into the press of people. A discordant yell of noise grew louder, seeming to splash a stronger stench of filth into Dex's nose as more ghosts from the surface of Triton stalked into view. The helmeted crossbow soldiers marched behind the knight. They wore red cloaks, their crossbows packed in leather bags, and they carried the big square shields on their backs.

The knight rode into the centre of the street, his horse's hooves splashing the stinking mud up round him. He looked round, sitting upright in his high-backed saddle and his steel-flashing face glaring around. In his steel-gloved hand he held a long lance, the butt hooked to his stirrup and the red-and-gold length sticking straight up to a sharp point. Buntings were strung over the street and the steel-man swung his lance sideways to avoid them. It hooked into the saint's halo and jerked it off, knocking the saint sideways. A howl of outrage arose from the crowd. The knight impatiently swung his horse round and the stamping hooves scattered muck. The black-robed man shouted with anger, flecks of the brown muck across his grey-bearded mouth. The knight wrenched his lance free and the saint fell sideways, face splintering under the hooves of his horse.

Another howl of outrage arose. Someone began a long calling shout and from everywhere, young men and boys in long leather aprons were running out of the narrow doorways. Dex was thrown sharply aside as a teenage boy, no older than him, with a mop of uncut hair and a pimpled red face, ran past. He was dressed in the same brown work-apron and carried a short thick stick. All the boys flung themselves on the knight and his soldiers, yelling with excitement and anger.

Beside Dex, an old man in a dirty white tunic and hood pushed himself back. A woman in a blue gown pulled her child into a doorway and a young man and woman, both clad in brown cloth, cannoned into Dex as they ran into the alley. In the street, the knight had dropped his lance and was swinging about him with one steel hand, trying to unhook a nasty-looking short steel club from his leather saddle bag as he did. But one of the leather-aproned boys, holding a pole with a sharp hook on the end, ducked under the horse's head. The boy raised the pole, hooking the point round the knight's steel-ridged shoulders and pulled hard. Steel feet were jerked from steel stirrups and with a flash of gilt and silver the metal-man crashed down into the centre of the brown ditch. More brown muck splashed up round him and his short steel club flew away and was trodden underfoot by the people suddenly crowding up from all sides. The crossbow soldiers were shouting, their helmets only covered to their noses, and Dex could see bearded lips snarling with anger as they spread out in a swirl of red cloaks. They were pulling the leather covers from their crossbows and Dex heard that trilling, and sensed the sudden thrill of danger as big stones began to fly through the air.

The teenage boys in leather aprons were bending down prising up the street stones and throwing them, their discordant shout a deafening yell of anger. The crossbow soldiers were firing their weapons, and pulling out long swords as the work-boys rushed up to them. A trumpet blast came from outside the street as Dex ran across, skidding in a pile of muck, a crossbow bolt burying itself in the plaster wall beside him. He crashed into a doorway but the door would not open.

The steel-man was on his knees, surrounded by yelling boys. All his bright armour was dulled with brown and his crossbow soldiers were trying to beat a way round him. Women leaned out of the upper windows, emptying pots of more brown muck on to them and the scream from everyone was deafening. The grey-bearded man in the black robe was pointing a skinny white finger, dancing up and down with anger and his eyes blazing with passion. Another bolt buried itself beside Dex, but most of the crossbow soldiers were in a tight circle, defending themselves against wooden clubs and stone missiles.

'Dex, you have to get out of here,' he said to himself.

Back across the road was another doorway. Beside it was a shuttered window and Dex threw himself back across the street. His boots skidded in the brown muck and two women banged into him, both about to throw stones. He slid between them and crawled over. Another leather-shoed foot banged painfully into his ribs, then he crawled forward and dived straight into it. Not the door, his instincts flashed, and he dived straight at the shuttered window. The wooden shutter broke and he crashed through into darkness. There was someone ahead; they collided and fell to the ground.

Dex got up, very angry. He knew he was covered with muck and that he stank like a blocked toilet. He was furious. It didn't matter if this person was a replica out of history, it was time to take it out on something. Dex rolled over, punching, but the replica person punched back. Dex felt himself hit hard and then thrown off. The other person stood up and he glimpsed mud-stained overalls.

'Dex!'

Asa grabbed his hand and pulled him up. Behind them, the noise, sunlight and confusion ended as though a brush were wiped across it. At the same time, the muck and stink seemed to evaporate off him and he looked round.

'Hey, what'd that force thing do with you?'

'Voyager showed me things.' Asa was shouting with an odd sense of triumph in her voice. 'Made me understand things.'

'Voyager?'

'Just watch!' she shouted again and a visual image storm broke round them in crashing beats of colour.

One moment giant tidal waves of a blazing yellow ocean were breaking round them. Then came an endless plain of jagged blue-grey rock, replaced by high mountains of dazzling ice. Exploding red volcanoes towered hundreds of kilometres high round churning red seas. Then a forest of high crystal needles, flashing purple, red and gold; a desert of orange silicate flakes under a yellow sky and two suns. A landscape of giant glaciers grinding and crunching into each other as though alive spreading through stone flatlands like giant ice-cold cobwebs. Each image flickered, melt-changing instantly into

149

the next, towering, crowding and flattening round them like a super-real hologram.

The images changed a last time to grey-blackness and this time it held, closing round them like one of the Earth history scenes. But this was another alien landscape. Dex knew it even before he felt sharp-edged pebbles underfoot and looked up at a strange star pattern in the black sky overhead.

'Where are we now?'

'Even an Earth kid should know that, Dex. Look!' She pointed up and now there was anger in her voice. 'We're looking at our solar system – in reverse. That near star is Pluto.'

A sense of incredulous wonder went through Dex like a power surge. This was the other side of a solar mirror. Planets like Pluto, Uranus and Neptune, almost unseen from Earth, were now bright and close. Earth was the unseen star and his incredulous wonder surged again because they could only be standing on one planet.

Stygnus. The new world beyond Pluto that Cleo had found.

Asa's voice was edged with triumph. 'Voyager was adjusted for some light, air and gravity. But this is *Stygnus!*'

Something large and heavy suddenly filled Dex's hands. It was a crossbow like those the medieval soldiers carried; a leather belt and bolt-pouch dragged at his waist. Asa held one too, a square leather pouch at her own hip. 'Hey, Asa, what're these things for?'

'To fight, Dex.' Her voice mocked in the silver-grey shadows. 'Voyager knows Earth people use weapons when they fight.'

'Who are we fighting?'

Asa pulled a bolt from her pouch and put it between her teeth. Then with a strange look at Dex, she began winding back the heavy steel bow of her weapon. She spoke from a full mouth, still with a determined edge of temper in her voice.

'Each other.'

17   A duel on cold Stygnus

Dex could sense the freezing temperature without feeling it. But there was another chill inside his own body as he watched Asa's strong hands winding back brass handles that pulled back the heavy cords and thick steel bow of her weapon.

'Asa, why does Voyager think we're going to fight?'

'Why shouldn't we?'

Her winding handle was click-click-clicking and Dex tried to make his own cold hands move. He pushed his boot into the metal stirrup under the bow, bracing it against the ground as he grabbed the icy brass handles and began jerking them round. And all the time he couldn't believe he was really doing it.

'Asa – why?'

A lot of reasons, thought Asa, and they were all flaming inside her. Something as strong as her fire was driving her, but she made her hands pause, speaking through the thick wooden bolt between her teeth.

'Look. Look down. Yes, look hard, Earth kid. Around you!'

Her metal bow stirrup scraped on the pebbly rock as Dex did as she said. Round him the grey-silver rocks stretched up into broken black shadows. The gleaming edges of starlight were reflected from them because the grey-silver surged everywhere in frozen streams and rivers of a dark flashing metal. Asa was standing on a low flat boulder that shone with a solid congealed gleam of dark silver.

Dex knew that metal at once, although it only existed through the asteroid belt in streaks, specks and tiny cobwebs hidden in the rock. He had nearly killed himself chasing through a hologram asteroid that was a duplicate of one riddled by a search for this metal. And now he was nearly getting himself killed again.

'Vulcanite,' came Asa's voice. 'The most precious thing in the solar system and we are standing on a planet of the stuff.'

'Asa, that's good— '

'Good— '

Her words came out with a rush as she pulled the bolt from her mouth. Dex hadn't finished rewinding or even pulled out his own bolt. But something in the way she spat the words out made Dex dive behind a rock, holding on to the crossbow with both hands.

'Asa – Asa!' he yelled. This rock also gleamed solid with vulcanite.

She didn't answer and there was a faint clattering of the sharp-edged pebbles as though she had begun rewinding again. Dex braced his foot in the metal stirrup and began turning the brass handles. Their clickety-click-click sounded threateningly loud in the stillness. He had a sense of tumbling headlong into something he couldn't understand. The crossbow was fully wound now and Dex fumbled in his leather pouch, pulling out one of the feathered bolts. Almost unconsciously he was following the actions of those crossbow soldiers who had fired on Castle Miranda.

'Dex, are you really this crazy?'

Asa's voice sounded all round him in the silver-black shadows. Dex looked carefully round because he heard the slight scattering of pebbles as Asa moved again.

'Why am I crazy? Everybody needs vulcanite!'

'Everybody?'

There was a sharp click and whizz. A crossbow bolt scored a sparking furrow of bright metal over the vulcanite rock. Dex ducked and moved into a deep gully, glinting edges of dark silver shadowing round him. He slotted the bolt in, just below the taut cord and let his finger touch the little brass trigger. This might be all a force-induced nightmare, but death was waiting now in the shadows. He had to find out where Asa was, make her start talking again.

'Yes, Asa, everyone, Earth— '

Another bolt skidded sharply overhead. Asa must have reloaded very quickly. And she had shot high, so maybe she was just trying to scare him. 'I'll tell you, Dex. *Earth* wants vulcanite more than we do. So there'll be more colonies, more cloning, maybe even different colours!'

She screamed the last word and Dex flinched, expecting another bolt. He kept moving deeper into the shadows. The ground sloped away here; he was in shadow and Asa was on the high ground. She would have to show herself to come down to him. He shouted again, raising the crossbow.

'Asa, we're *all* from Earth— '

'No!' That scream again and another bolt skittered overhead. 'I am from Pallas and the gas giants are *our* side of the solar system. Nothing belongs to that dead planet you call Earth!' Under her words he could hear the scrabbling of pebbles and a faint click-click as she reloaded the crossbow.

Dex was angry now. *Nobody* was going to shoot at him like that. He jumped up, glimpsing Asa outlined against the starlight, bending over the crossbow as she fitted an arrow. He pressed the brass trigger, firing blindly, the bow jerking upward and the wooden butt thumping against his shoulder. Then he ducked back and Asa's voice came again as though nothing had happened.

'Where will the next colonies be?' Her words glinted with rage like the sharp-edged rocks. 'Titania, Umbriel – Miranda?' Maybe it was the last, a moon of Uranus and the name of their linker, but another bolt scraped over the rocks, sparking vulcanite in the blackness.

Dex bent and picked up a handful of gleaming pebbles. He started throwing them back up the gully, one at a time as he moved deeper into the blackness. Asa would hear them, think they were his footsteps and be watching in the wrong direction. So he could come up behind and – he felt the bow click back, fitting another arrow – then he would have to decide what to do.

'Asa. Earth won't do things like that any more. Nobody thinks like that now. There's only the World Council now and everybody's important.' He was shouting the words into the blackness and threw another pebble, even further. 'You're hung up on the past – think about the future!'

'The past is what made me, Rainie.'

So he was back to being a Rainie again. But her voice was more distant, so maybe his trick was working. A Rainie can outsmart a Rockie any day of the week, he nearly shouted back, but it was time to keep silent now. He slipped further around the rock and found it was bottoming out in a narrow valley. Bizarre silver-grey shapes were growing in the blackness as though once, long ago, liquid vulcanite had spouted and frozen in twisting mushroom-topped shapes. They spiralled and looped round and over him and Dex felt sharp edges rip his track suit as he squeezed past. Where the valley sloped up, stems of vulcanite outlined a deep cleft in the rock. From there, his back and sides protected, he could wait for Asa to show herself.

Asa hadn't shouted again, but she was out there somewhere and might now be getting close. The mushroom heads of vulcanite overshadowed him in the darkness and he nearly hooked his crossbow on a jutting stem. His feet slipped on a smooth metal patch beneath him and then he was at the cleft. Even in this tense moment, he could marvel at how the vulcanite twisted round the cleft like a scrolled silver archway. And all of this was made fantastically real only by the Triton force. Dex looked round. There was no sign of Asa, no sound, so he had time to decide what to do. Lifting the crossbow, Dex backed into the cleft.

Something cold and metallic touched the back of his neck and Dex stopped rigid. Vulcanite, he thought for a moment, then it moved slightly. It was the brass stirrup of a crossbow and at this range the arrow bolt would go through his neck. Behind him, Asa's voice hissed with rage and triumph.

'I was born on rocks like these, Rainie. Now drop it.'

Dex opened his hands and let the crossbow fall. The bowstring twanged and his bolt skittered off among the stems of vulcanite. And if Asa's finger on the crossbow trigger was as tense as her voice, then he had to make himself speak calmly.

'What happens now, Asa?'

'Why, what did you have planned, Dex?' The crossbow was hard and cold against his neck.

'You loaded your crossbow first!'

'Voyager told me to.'

'Voyager— ' Dex felt the crossbow move a little away as though even Asa realised how crazy it sounded. He took a step forward and kicked his crossbow away. Then, with his hands half-raised, he turned round, stepping back again and letting Asa come out of the cleft after him. She did so, the crossbow half-lifted but one hand firmly over the trigger. Her eyes glittered in the dark silver starlight. He swallowed and tried not to look scared or let his voice shake.

'Asa, what is this Voyager? And why is it showing us all these things? Maybe it wants us to fight, like all those people in history.'

'Voyager knows all about Earth emotion, Dex.' Her voice was as cold and dark as the rocks round them and her hands stayed steady and tight on the crossbow. 'And human nature. And it *knows* what Earth will do to get that vulcanite!'

'Do we have to talk about it here?' Dex took another step back and nearly tripped on a dark silver stem. 'Asa, you've got some kind of link with this thing— '

'I've got more than that.' Asa's eyes flashed and there was that savage triumph in her voice. 'Voyager *knows* me, Voyager has *accepted* me in a way you'll never understand.'

157

'Then prove it.' Dex knew he was scared now – that savage glittery note was too strong in Asa's voice. 'Show me Earth hasn't changed.'

'Yes Dex, I'll show you. But first I'll tell you what Voyager is.'

Asa raised a hand in the air and seemed to clutch something invisible. Then she pulled it down and it was as though she was pulling the darkness down with her.

18   Doorway into darkness

The scene melt-changed. Dark silver metal, black rocks and grey starlight swirled smoothly together and separated themselves again into different outlines as though poured into an invisible mould. They were back in the waiting area again; his track suit was still torn and Asa held her crossbow. His own lay on the floor. Dex unbuckled the leather belt and pouch and let it fall down. After a moment, Asa did the same, but one-handed because she was still holding her crossbow ready.

'Will it try to kill us again?'

Dex, are you listening to yourself? Asa thought. Do you know how scared you sound because of that play-acting on Stygnus? Voyager wouldn't let us kill each other. I *know* Voyager. I know because I can feel Voyager inside me the way you never will. Voyager has told me its story as simply and clearly as pouring water into a glass. Her voice sounded very clear and strong to her, even though she had the feeling her lips were not moving. Her unspoken words rang in the coffee-darkness and she knew Dex could hear every word.

At first it had been difficult to understand Voyager; perhaps just as difficult for Voyager to understand her because Voyager was created to store data, not contact alien life-forms. It was created by an alien race far across the universe in a triple-sun galaxy.

Even billions of years ago, they were millions of years advanced on Earth. And they decided to chart the universe the way Earth once charted its continents.

Their probe was a giant moon-sized sphere with a bio-mass of intelligence and energy banks recharging from every solar system it passed through. And it had circled the universe, criss-crossing its own path, section by section, storing data about every planet in every galaxy, atmosphere, mineral content and anywhere there was a life-form. All the data was faithfully transmitted back to its alien masters, all of it able to be recreated in solid force imagery.

Then the home planet was destroyed, said Asa in her spoken loud thoughts. Voyager sensed a burning as though its makers were super-novaed in the heat of their own exploding suns. So Voyager went into hold. It circled the nearest planet – Neptune – but in an irregular, uneven orbit because it wasn't a real moon. Thinking for perhaps another million years then becoming attracted to the tiny swarming life-forms on the third planet from this sun.

Her thoughts now had the lonely edge of all those orbiting, endless centuries. In that time, Voyager became fascinated by humans. Humans were different from anything it had seen because they had emotions. Voyager was drawn to emotion and how it changed, from peace to anger, happiness to rage. And when the android-remotes came here, it tried to make contact. It sent up life-forms it thought we would know about. And when *we* arrived it did the same thing. It tried to get the humans down, but in its own clumsy way, like jabbing someone with pins to get their attention. Then it showed us those recreations to try and match up the

160

different levels of emotion in our minds. Then open our minds.

Yes, Asa, whispered the voice deep inside and Asa switched off the Dex-wavelength she was speaking on and said the next thoughts only to herself. That there were things even Voyager didn't understand because the aliens had built no maturity into Voyager. It was just a big kid and grown many times older than it ever should have, understanding both too much and not enough, and always feeling an intense loneliness.

Yes, Asa, said the voice again.

'How does it make those re-creations?' said Dex.

Asa wasn't even sure if he'd heard all that. 'Dex, could you explain hi-tech lasers to those crossbow soldiers?' Without thinking, she rested the crossbow on a chair but kept her hand on it. And her fingers tightened again as she heard Dex's next words.

'So that power surge was a contact signal, but – but too strong. Jona, Tieve and the others – Asa, it was an accident.'

'Yes, Dex.' Her index finger touched the brass trigger again. 'But Earth and Mars Orbit blamed us – remember?' He did remember; she could see the sudden dismay in his face.

There was silence again round them. Dex knew Asa had scored and she was still standing in that tense way, one hand on the crossbow. And round them, the tiny underneath trill of power had begun again. Voyager, he thought, can sense the emotion building and is fascinated.

'Asa, we made a mistake, that's all. Earth and the World Council are not monsters out to destroy –' he nearly said Tints and bit his tongue, '– the solar colonies.' Suddenly it was as if that trilling sound

161

sent another power surge through him. 'OK, Asa! If Voyager caused this, then Voyager recorded it.'

Asa paused. Her eyes still flashed as they had in the dark silver shadows of Stygnus, but her hand on the crossbow relaxed uncertainly.

Dex tried hard to keep an edge of triumph out of his own voice. 'Then Voyager can give us a playback!' His voice rang for a moment and the trilling stopped. Asa wasn't looking at him but over his shoulder, and the glare had gone from her eyes.

Dex knew before he turned that she was looking at the doorway.

'Dex, we don't have to go through that door.'

Now Asa's voice sounded uncertain. Perhaps because this time *he* had called up Voyager and not her. The door was shut and quiet, but somehow gleamed with a quiet waiting truth behind it, the truth about Earth and the solar colonies that Asa was afraid to face.

'Can't you just listen to me, Dex?'

'Let's both listen to the truth.'

He wasn't afraid of Asa and her crossbow any more. She couldn't use an old-fashioned weapon like that to hide reality. Dex turned his back on her and walked over to the door. He opened it and this time the artificial glowing light of MarsOrbit came through. Without waiting to see if Asa would follow, Dex walked through into his own world.

Even knowing about solid holograms didn't prepare him for this. Dex gasped and took a step back because the reality hit him like a punching force. He was looking at himself, in the Spoke console room and Romhilda was on screen before him.

Him. He was looking at himself, a different person.

162

No, Dex thought to himself, this guy isn't me, I don't talk like that. I don't stand with my hands on my hips and swagger, I don't talk with my mouth curled, my voice all flip and arrogant. No, that's not me!

'Bloody Rockies! OK, we need Tints, but who the hell gave them brains? My friends got bounced because of those two jerks— '

His voice continued behind him, but Dex turned, shouting over it. 'Asa I was different then, I was scared, I didn't understand – that's not the way I am now!'

'No, Dex.' Asa was standing in the black outline of the doorway, crossbow in hand. Then it slid shut behind her. 'But *that* is the way *Earth* is now.'

One hand, complete with crossbow, pointed. Dex turned, hearing a door shut, knowing the other Dex had gone. The other Dex had kicked his way back to his space sleep to listen to Friedelinde's soothing tones again.

'You heard all that?' Romhilda said behind them.

'Yes, I heard all that,' said a voice Dex knew.

He turned again. Another person had entered the replica room. Jahudi, down from the upper tiers of Spoke. There was no smile on his thin brown face and his lips were set in a hard line as Romhilda turned and spoke.

'So we're going to blame the Martians – again.'

'Why not?' Jahudi did smile now, but it was unpleasant and showed a gleam of white teeth. 'That'll teach them to bring in Rockies from Pallas.'

Behind him Dex heard Asa gasp, but now he didn't dare turn round. He was trembling, not because this was bad but because he knew there was worse to come. Jahudi walked over, spun the console chair where only a few minutes earlier Conleth's body had been, and sat down.

'The colonies are becoming restive.' Another gleam of white teeth showed. 'We don't need a repeat of five years ago.' That was when the colonies stopped mineral shipments to Earth until they were given control of their bases. 'Now they want terraforming.'

'I thought they were getting it,' said Romhilda.

It *was* Romhilda speaking and this *was* the console deck, every detail perfect, real and alive. Dex watched with a growing sense of horror, rigid, aware of Asa's glaring presence behind him as Jahudi sat back in the chair, his eyes as cold as the grey-silver-rock of Stygnus.

'Earth priorities come first,' said Jahudi. 'We need the colonies to be dependant on us. Terraforming will give them too much . . .' his teeth gleamed again 'independence.'

'And something like this helps keep them in line, right?' said Romhilda. There was tension in her voice and something else – disgust. 'So they forget about terraforming for a time.'

'Your report will stress that, Romhilda.'

'I am tired of my reports stressing the wrong things.'

Jahudi was silent for a moment, but his thin lips moved in an even more unpleasant smile. 'Your family on Earth must be looking forward to your return.'

Dex heard himself choke again, then he was pushed aside as Asa walked past to the centre of the room, between Jahudi and Romhilda, hair disarranged round her face and eyes glaring as she looked from one to the other.

'You know I have to get back to Earth,' Romhilda had said over this. The disgust was stronger in her voice. 'And this won't help because other people know— '

'Only Dexter and the Rockie.' Jahudi stood up, looking with those stone eyes right through Asa's resolute, hate-filled glare. 'We'll send them to Neptune. Perfect because that Cleo wants an all-Tint crew. Chances are none of them will come back.' He began walking to the door.

'Isn't that clever of us?' said Romhilda.

It was her turn to look unseeingly into Asa's hating stare and something of it showed in her own eyes. But her look was from time and images recorded months before. As was Jahudi's in his reply. 'Earth comes first, Romhilda. Always.'

The door slid shut on Jahudi's thin smile and Romhilda went over to sit in one of the console chairs – Phyllida's. But she slumped and put black hands over her black face and sat without moving, seeming to become part of the unmoving background.

'Dex!'

He had never heard such rage and hate in a human voice. It screamed and echoed round the room and all of the time seemed to slow. The room rippled in closing circles round Asa, then round the crossbow and her hand on the trigger. Then her finger tightened and the sharp-pointed crossbow bolt leapt at him from the twanging cord.

19   Battle in the mind

Asa didn't know why her finger squeezed tight so suddenly. The anger was hot and boiling, and if she fired anywhere else the bolt would just bounce back – the way everything bounced off a steel-thick uncaring Earth. But as it flashed towards Dex, she screamed again and the noise seemed to slow the speeding bolt. She was as bad as *them* and she didn't want Dex to die. The bolt slowed again and Asa's mind raged at her. That was *their* solution – Voyager, save me!

Asa heard herself scream. Then those ripples closed even further, round the speeding bolt like layers of glass, slowing it down. But it struck Dex. In slow motion Asa saw it cut through his tunic and the force of the blow threw him back, arms outspread and the bolt sticking in his chest.

No, *please* Voyager!

Asa screamed to herself and shut her eyes as Dex crashed to the floor. She had just killed someone who saved her life, who meant something to her. But the other side of her mind came back like a bitter raging flood – *Earth* did this, not her. The hate flooded through her body and round her, the trilling harmonics reached a high pitch. Asa knelt, star horizons whirling round, and she battled her emotions – cold water splashing over hot rocks, heat and ice colliding with each other, super-novaed suns blotting out life on a planet far away. She had to

166

focus, push, let the ice-blue flame meet the white-hot one; Asa screamed again with agony because she knew she had to win this battle over herself, over the same emotions that still drove Cleo and Lan.

She was on her knees and the red-black solar-storm beat round her. Then it died down; the blue flames spread over the red ones and all that boiling rage began to die down. Asa knew she had won before she opened her eyes. Dex was still lying flat with the bolt sticking in his chest. Then he sat up and the bolt, held only by the fabric of his tunic, fell sideways. The darkness came back down, but this time it was different.

Asa and Dex could still see each other. But there was a choking black stench round them and the ground became wet and soggy as Dex scrambled to his feet. For the moment their quarrel, the anger and betrayal of that recorded scene were forgotten as the darkness lifted.

'What planet is this?' breathed Dex, choking again as a fetid thick smell swirled in a greasy mist round him.

Asa dropped her crossbow and it splotched into a sickly green pool. Ahead a bank stretched down, further and further into darkness that opened before them like a gigantic meteor crater. The sky was red-black overhead and they turned. Almost over-head, a huge mass of crystal humped itself out of the ground, the broken irregular facets flashing the dying red-blackness. But even worse than this and the stench was the awful silence that spread round them, more black and dead than anything they saw.

'This is the last vision of Voyager,' said Asa.

Her words died as she spoke them because nothing

could live in this desolate red-black gloom, even sounds. Everything here was dead and Asa shut her eyes as the darkness came down again.

'Won, Asa, won,' said the voice.

'Yes, won,' she repeated without understanding.

She was saying it aloud and opened her eyes again. That terrible rotting stink was still in her mouth and nose but her first breath sent cool cleansing power fire through her body. There was a soft caress on her cheeks; walls, floor and ceiling were nothing but dark beautiful flames, fire that burned blue, violet and crimson then mixed into a colour unknown; it shimmered, rippled and beat round her like gentle strong waves and Asa knew she was standing inside the soul of Triton, the bio-electronic creature she called Voyager.

'Get Dex back,' she whispered, unconsciously falling into the baby-talk of Voyager.

'Not yet. Need you first. For me.'

'For you . . .' The glowing dark mass drowned through her as she spoke in sonic wavebeats. 'To help you . . . save you . . .?'

'No Asa. Other way.'

'I don't understand.' But she was beginning to, because the flame was burning strongly inside her.

'Back to ship. You for me, not others. Must die, Asa.'

'Who . . .' she whispered, knowing. 'Who is going to die?'

Dex came slowly out of the darkness on to a solid floor that seemed to heave and rock, and pressed coldly against his face. Something clanged like a hatch shutting and he rolled over, wincing as he opened his eyes into a sharp overhead dazzle of light. Asa was shouting at him.

'Dex, get up!'

'We're not going anywhere,' he muttered. What was Asa talking about? They were black-glued somewhere under the surface of Triton.

'Yes we are – the bow section is taking off again!'

The floor angled sharply and Dex jerked suddenly awake as he slid across. A crashing jar went through the linker and he picked himself up. Asa was already staggering down the passage to the control room and he followed. The linker shook again, sideways from wall to wall, then forward into the control room.

'Strap in!' Asa yelled.

The room rocked again as Dex threw himself into the second chair and fumbled with the straps. Then, with a last thud, the blackness ran in streaks from the observation port and the bow section broke itself free from the ice. Pink snow swirled round the windows and cleared. Without any apparent power, they were rocketing up through the layers of methane and below, a mass of pink snow drifted away from Triton's ice-cap.

'Going up?' he whispered.

'Voyager is sending us back into space,' said Asa without looking at him. She leaned back in Cleo's big chair. 'It didn't do much talking. All it said was— '

She broke off and sat up against the strap, gasping. Dex looked ahead too, into the blue-blackness of outer space. Of all the impossible things they had seen, this was the least expected and the most incredible. Because towards them, at a steady glide and still in orbit, came the stern section of Link Miranda.

'Has Voyager finished with us?' said Dex.

'I don't know,' said Asa.' She did know of course. Voyager had told her what to do and her thoughts were as cold and dark as Stygnus rock. They were thoughts of death.

20 Death wish

Under her deep-sleep unit, Cleo stirred uneasily. She had set the stern section co-ordinates to turn out of Triton's orbit and Mars would be ahead when she woke. Then she had gone into deep sleep and begun her favourite dream – the one that went beyond Pluto, out, out into the further darkness of Stygnus, further than any human since the dawn of time. And Earth would never know the secrets of Stygnus; they belonged to outer space and the next generation of blue, red and green genetic solar people like her.

She could feel herself being carried. This wasn't part of the dream and she tried to break free of it. But she could hear a voice, Asa who was gone, telling her it was all right; she could feel herself being settled in her command chair, but that was just a dream because the command chair and Asa, who she loved like a daughter, were gone. The straps round her, the close re-fitting of her deep-sleep unit and Asa's soothing voice, were all part of the dream.

'Dream and be happy,' came Asa's soft, whispering voice.

And now she was floating back into the darkness, at the controls of Link Miranda with the cold black rock of Stygnus ahead. She could forget the unhappy blankness of not knowing where she was from and her hate of the Earth system that gave her life for the wrong reasons. Because Earth was only a star in the blackness and the whole wonderful galaxy called her like a mother.

Dex leaned wearily against the second chair. 'I thought she was going to wake for a moment,' he said.

'She nearly did,' said Asa. 'Settled now.'

Link Miranda was whole again. Triton's unseen force had guided the two halves neatly together, fusing them in a single fire-sealing moment so completely that no trace of the join remained.

'Get a shower and change,' she said abruptly. 'Then we'll talk.'

Dex went. That Triton force was still round them, he knew, because he could walk normally in the artificial gravity it was somehow generating. It had let them move quickly, carrying first Lan to his front deep-sleep position, them Cleo. Both were so completely in their deep sleep that there was just time to settle them before they awoke. Rek's deep-sleep unit was always in the rear so they left him there; Dex was relieved because the big muscular boy looked as though he weighed a tonne. Round them, the linker hummed into full life.

Asa was still standing by the command chair when he came back, looking down at Triton and Neptune. 'I'm sorry about firing that crossbow,' she said. 'What those people said – it was just too much.' Her face was hard and frowning a little as though she'd come to a decision she didn't like.

Dex had been coming to a set of decisions too. 'Asa, I think all that vulcanite will change things. I really do. Earth won't have to be so – selfish.'

'Or maybe Earth will get worse.' Asa spoke as

though she had already answered the same questions in her own mind.

'Then I'll let you decide. I won't say anything. I'll even stay on Mars if you want me to. Dex felt angry with himself at the way he said that, for it sounded too self-sacrificing. He *did* want to stay on Mars with Asa.

Asa tried to smile, but there was too much sadness. If only Dex had said this earlier. 'I believe you Dex. And *you* believe it too – now.'

'Forever, Asa,' he said, because she had to believe that. And he was so relieved to see her nod and smile.

'Forever.' She held out her hand and Dex took it. Asa squeezed tight and the sadness came into her voice. 'Dex, it has to be forever.'

She brought out her other hand. He just had time to see the tiny metal tube in her fingers, then it tingled through his body. Everything went weak and numb and he would have collapsed if Asa hadn't held him so tightly, lowering him gently to the floor. Anaesthetic from the medical kit, a big dose that was paralysing and deadening his whole body. He tried to open his mouth, but he couldn't move his tongue.

'You can't speak Dex. Don't try.'

Her voice was very gentle. She bent and picked Dex up in her arms; he could feel the strength of her body as she carried him quickly down to his cabin and set him on the bed. Her hands moved just as quickly over his body, strapping him in and adjusting the deep-sleep unit. Then she sat on the edge of the bed and turned his head so that they were looking at each other.

'I am a young woman of Pallas. I am of outer space,

not Earth. That is why I am doing what I have to.' Her voice stumbled, sounding a little apologetic but always firm. 'Do you remember all those recreations of the past that Voyager showed us? And that last one before we came up, of that black and dead planet?' Her hands tightened on his. 'That was *Earth* Dex. Voyager has seen too much of the universe to be wrong. Voyager has assessed survival chances for Earth. They are nil. Earth is too far gone, whatever is done now, *finished*.'

Asa, no, that doesn't have to be true. The vulcanite will save us, at least make us last longer. But Dex's words stayed on his tongue. Asa shook his hands as though to say no to his thoughts and kept talking.

'The vulcanite won't save Earth – nothing can, because you can't change human nature and it's too late. You heard Jahudi and Romhilda. They won't change any more than Cleo will. So I have to think about tomorrow. About the new solar system, not the old Earth. About *my* generation and *our* chances. Not letting Earth strip solar resources just as they stripped their planet of rain forests.'

Dex was still trying to speak, but blackness was creeping round him like an ambush. He saw the glint of a tear as Asa adjusted the deep-sleep unit down. His tongue still wouldn't move and her voice was a silver wire in the dark as the sonic hum of the unit began.

'I'm sorry, Dex. Goodbye.'

Now the electronic blackness was humming open in his mind and he was shouting, no Asa, we can do this together, I won't let . . . But he was shouting the words inside his mouth, then only in his mind and the sonic blackness drowned everything, even Asa's tight hands still holding his.

Asa sat beside Dex for a long time before she took her hands away. Then she got up and went through to the control room again and brought up all the deep-sleep units on-screen. She could feel Voyager's own scanning force tingling round her and knew she only had to speak each name and all memory of the last five days would be wiped clean.

'Rek.' He wasn't bright enough to keep his mouth shut. 'Lan.' One glass of boot juice and he would be telling everyone. 'Cleo.' That hurt almost as much as the next would. Cleo was too bright and still would tell too many people. Then the last name. 'Dex.'

It's not the vulcanite, Dex. Earth cannot know about Voyager because Voyager is giving me something too important. The brain-wave lines smoothed out and it was over. None of them would remember. She went over to the window and looked down at the blue mass of Triton, a section of Neptune's banded rings and the blue-green mass of the planet itself beyond that. The quiet voice spoke in her mind, but so distinctly that she heard it in the cabin round her.

'End now, Asa. Time for death.'

'Yes, I'm ready.'

Asa tensed herself. She had never felt more young or more vulnerable, and this was the most terrible moment of her life. But she had gone too far and it was going to happen. She tensed and spread her arms wide, opening out her hands and screaming as a sudden sharp pain stabbed and burned into each palm like laser nails. Intense streaks of fire ran up

175

her arms and through both sides of her body, fusing together in her brain with a last blinding flash. It was new life, new intelligence – and she fought back another scream as it burned hotly, the laser fire still streaming from each hand. The voice spoke again in a tired closing way.

'Goodbye Asa.'

Asa was almost afraid to speak, as though the new energy would flame out of her mouth if she did. And below her, Triton shuddered and began moving down in a descending spiral towards the massive blue-green surface of Neptune. Slowly, then more quickly, but always controlled because Asa knew that even dying, Voyager would not put its mother planet a metre out of orbit.

The energy surge had subsided now, but it still bubbled hotly in her body and shimmered like a halo round her. Voyager's own bio-energy was given to her because the space probe was billions of years older than its dead makers, because it had lived too long and seen too much. Below, a huge cloud of steam arose on Neptune's surface and Asa sensed something stopping, something dying. Her hands were still outstretched and she raised them over her head, feeling the energy force lock between them. Her tears boiled on hot cheeks and she breathed out the fire force and passion of her new strength; she only whispered, but knew the mysterious wonderful thing would hear as it slipped into blackness.

'Goodbye, Voyager.'

21 Ghost morning

'You're just not safe anywhere, Cadet Dexter,' said Romhilda. 'Even Triton takes a dive into Neptune to avoid you.'

She was smiling though, as much as Dex had seen that chubby apple face ever smile. Behind the closed doors of the waiting area, the huge Earth-linker was vibrating with life as it came to take-off power. Soon they would be boarding and after a few weeks of deep-sleep, he would be on Earth. And Jahudi, after all the smiles and congratulations at his safe return, assured him that Friedelinde had not forgotten him.

Dex nodded and tried to smile back at Romhilda, wishing a tiny corner of memory would stop flicking at the edge of his mind. This was the morning of departure and he should be excited, impatient to go home. But that little ghost memory kept flickering.

He hadn't seen Asa since Link Miranda docked. She had gone to a new hi-tech South Quadrant and hadn't answered his post-spark. She was in his dreams, though; they were both among bizarre people in fantastic costumes, on starlit black floors and a chaos of different planets. They were crazy dreams, but every night they faded a little more even though that tiny edge of memory flickered whenever he thought of Asa. And Triton, the word hung in his mind like a ghost.

'You've changed a lot.' Romhilda was eyeing him closely.

'Triton did that,' he said.

Romhilda looked puzzled and after a moment, so did Dex. *Why* should he say that? Triton had stopped existing, apparently falling away from its uneven backwards orbit before they were out of deep-sleep. A one in a million solar calamity and they had missed it. But the tel-spark was in place and it was rather nice to sit here and know all the other cadets going home on rotate were eyeing him with hero worship because he had been to Neptune and back. Even Romhilda seemed pleased he had returned. The waiting area door opened and Dex glimpsed a red-brown skinned worker enter. One of the cadets yelled over at once.

'Wrong shuttle, Tint!'

'Shut-up! They're people like us!' That was *him* shouting and Dex couldn't believe it, or explain the sudden anger.

The cadet just gaped, then the boarding call came and the access doors to their linker slid open. Romhilda got up and came over, speaking just over the upbeat of the engines. 'Yes, you have changed.' This time she actually did smile and nodded back as she headed for the access. 'I think that's for you.'

Dex turned. The red-brown skinned Solie was Asa, standing just inside the door. 'I just came to say goodbye.' She was looking at him carefully, in a secret appraising way. 'I hear you're going to the new sea city.'

Dex nodded, then blinked a little. He'd dreamed about a sea city last night, but it was a horrible dream of a humped broken mass; so destroyed it looked like a natural formation of quartzite, by the shores of a dry ocean under a red-black sky. Just a bad dream, though, because Earth was over its problems now.

'Yes,' he said. The ghost memory flickered again and the boarding call was repeated behind them. There was so much he should be saying to Asa, but nothing he could remember.

'I'm joining a terraforming unit at Orduna Set, south-east Mars,' she said with that careful secret look. 'We've got good ideas and we're going to make things work. Real skies, real weather.'

'Real rainbows?' said Dex. He meant it to be a joke but that awful ghost memory caught at the words again.

'Real rainbows.' Asa nodded and smiled tightly. 'Goodbye, Dex.'

'Goodbye, Asa.'

He put out his hand and Asa squeezed it tight. Dex knew there was another time she'd squeezed his hands, but it was lost in memory-blackness. So he just smiled and turned abruptly for the linker access. Then he spun round again because something screamed *don't go*, but that was crazy, just nerves. He raised his hand and Asa lifted her own red-brown one in a farewell gesture as the doors slid shut between them.

He doesn't remember, Asa thought, so the secrets are safe. So I can't even thank him for saving my life, even for shouting at that stupid cadet. But you did shout, Dex, that's something. And I can't tell you my secrets, though I want to. Because what Voyager told me in the moment it died is just too awesome.

There was another alien moon in the solar system. A data-gatherer that Voyager had sent out, and that was now lost somewhere. I can find it and use the special power it has, she thought, but I must be very careful because there can be no more mistakes.

The waiting area vibrated as the long-linker began moving away on to the launching ramp. Asa stood there, telling herself to forget Dex, forget everything but the days of real rainbows. She closed both hands tight and smiled again as that wonderful fire force coursed through her body again. It was like a glowing warm fire that never went out and one day Asa knew it would flare gloriously and tell her what to do.

Dex was standing by a big porthole in the cargo hold. The linker was already twenty thousand kilometres out and he should be in his cubicle, preparing for deep-sleep, but he was watching the big red planet of Mars, already framed by black space. There were ghost memories flickering in his mind and he wanted to hold on to them. The first instruction to deep-sleep came, then the second. The third had his name on it, uttered in the sharp tones of the Earth pilot himself.

Then the porthole closed and Dex went to his cubicle and lay down. He began to adjust his deep-sleep unit. The ghost memories still crowded, of Asa and something fantastic they shared; of Triton, the moon that no longer was. The memories were sad and they were fading and Dex knew that when he woke up on Earth, they would be gone.

DEEPWATER BLACK

Ken Catran

There's an enemy on her spaceship and Yoona needs Robbie to fight it. But Robbie's from Earth – he doesn't belong on a spaceship thousands of years in the future.

Or does he?

What precious cargo does Deepwater carry in her hidden chambers? Who set her on an unknown course? And what has happened to Earth?

Robbie and Yoona must find the enemy set on destroying the spaceship. Then they'll know the truth about their mission.

And the horrifying secret about themselves.

2 DEEPWATER LANDING
Far from Earth. Far from home. Only one girl can save the mission.

3 DEEPWATER ANGELS
They thought it was over. But now they face the final challenge . . .

DOOMFIRE ON VENUS

Ken Catran

Jily Tennoto's life is about to change. She has been selected to join a top-secret unit with two other trainees. They are to be sent to the most terrifying planet of all: Venus – the Hell Planet.

Here Jily makes a mind-boggling discovery. A discovery that could save Earth, but destroy Jily and her companions.

Because Venus has a secret as old as time itself.

And time is running out.

SHADOW OF PHOBOS

Ken Catran

Cela, a Martian colonist, is kidnapped and taken to Earth. Telesforo, an Earth-boy on an urgent mission, crash-lands on Mars. Now, both teenagers are being stalked by an unknown killer.

One thing links them.

Something that will wake horrors long since forgotten.

Something that will change the solar system for ever.

KEN CATRAN
Published by Hodder Children's Books

62672 0	Deepwater Black	£2.99	☐
62673 9	Deepwater Landing	£2.99	☐
62674 7	Deepwater Angels	£2.99	☐
63484 7	Doomfire on Venus	£2.99	☐
63485 5	The Ghosts of Triton	£2.99	☐
63486 3	Shadow of Phobos	£2.99	☐

All Hodder Children's books are available at your local bookshop or newsagent, or can be ordered direct from the publisher. Just tick the titles you want and fill in the form below. Prices and availability subject to change without notice.

Hodder Children's Books, Cash Sales Department, Bookpoint, 39 Milton Park, Abingdon, OXON, OX14 4TD, UK. If you have a credit card you may order by telephone – (01235) 831700.

Please enclose a cheque or postal made payable to Bookpoint Ltd to the value of the cover price and allow the following for postage and packing:
UK & BFPO – £1.00 for the first book 50p for the second book, and 30p for each additional book ordered up to a maximum charge of £3.00.
OVERSEAS & EIRE – £2.00 for the first book, £1.00 for the second book, and 50p for each additional book.

Name ....
Address...
....
....
If you would prefer to pay by credit card, please complete:
Please debit my Visa/Access/Diner's Card/American Express (delete as applicable) card no:

Signature ....
Expiry Date...